# The Broken Bridge

## THE FALL AND ATONEMENT

### MIKE CLEVELAND

SETTING CAPTIVES FREE PUBLISHING

The Broken Bridge paperback
ISBN: 978-1-968656-00-3

The Broken Bridge hardback
ISBN: 978-1-968656-01-0

The Broken Bridge Kindle
ISBN: 978-1-968656-02-7

The Broken Bridge Audiobook
ISBN: 978-1-968656-03-4

# Contents

Best Seller                                                                    V

Editorial Review                                                               VI
by Literary Titan

What Readers Are Saying About The Broken Bridge                              VIII
Early Reader Reviews and Testimonials

Acknowledgments                                                                IX
With Deep Gratitude

About the Author                                                               XI
Mike Cleveland

1.  The Great Bridge                                                            1
    Where Two Shores Become one

2.  When The Earth Shook                                                        8
    Foundations Undone

3.  Across The Divide                                                          14
    Signals Through Darkness

4.  Regulus                                                                    21
    The Law-Maker

5.  Sophia                                                                     35
    The Philosopher

6. Ritus      48
   The Ritualist

7. Altruia      59
   The Helper

8. Optimus      69
   The Self-Believer

9. Metamorphia      80
   The Changer

10. Hope Deferred      91
    Makes The Heart Sick

11. The Ordinary One      99
    Geshriel's Life

12. The Teacher      112
    Geshriel's Teaching

13. The True Foundation      126
    Geshriel's Love And Sacrifice

14. The Keystone of Love      139
    Geshriel's Accomplishment

15. The Reunion      151
    What Love Restored

16. Author's Note      160

17. Before The Bridge Was Built      162
    A Preview of The Living Bridge

# Best Seller

T he Broken Bridge was an Amazon number one new release, and number one best seller in Christian Fiction/Fantasy.

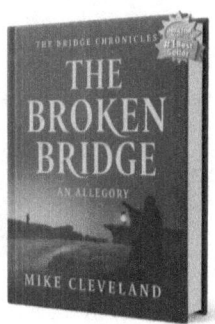

*Amazon Number One Best Seller*

# Editorial Review

## BY LITERARY TITAN

M ike Cleveland's *The Broken Bridge* is a sweeping allegorical tale about unity lost and the sacrificial love that alone can restore it. The story begins in a vibrant and harmonious world where two communities are joined by the Great Bridge. More than just stone and mortar, it's a living heart that binds people together. Fidel and Verita's love is set to be sealed at the bridge's center, but a sudden and catastrophic collapse shatters both the structure and the people's trust. As the physical chasm grows, so does the spiritual and moral divide, giving way to fear, selfishness, and grief. Various figures, each embodying different philosophies and approaches, arrive to offer their versions of repair, but only one path leads toward true restoration. Through vivid scenes and a layered cast of characters, Cleveland builds an allegory of the human condition, the Fall, and the atonement.

The imagery is lush but never indulgent; the bridge itself is practically a character, breathing with history and meaning. Cleveland's gift lies in his ability to make a symbolic world feel tangible. I could smell the bread from the communal kitchens, hear the lapping of the Vitae River, and feel the stone vibrate under the feet of a united people. When disaster struck, the grief was palpable. He writes loss in a way that made my chest ache. And yet, there's a steady thread of hope woven in, even through the darker passages, that kept me turning pages long after midnight.

The book isn't just a pleasant walk through metaphor. It has sharp edges. The portrayal of human frailty, how quickly love can curdle into self-preservation, hits uncomfortably close to home. I found myself frustrated with characters who gave up too soon, and pained by those who clung to impossible ideals, hurting others in the process. There were moments I wanted to shout advice into the pages. But that's a credit to Cleveland's storytelling; his people aren't cardboard saints or villains. They're complex, flawed, and deeply human. At times, the moral symbolism is overt, but it never feels like a sermon being read to you. It feels like a mirror being held up.

*The Broken Bridge* left me with that rare mix of satisfaction and longing. The sense that the story had resolved, but that its truths would keep echoing long afterward. It's a tale for readers who enjoy their fiction with meaning baked into every scene, who don't mind being made uncomfortable on the way to being inspired. I'd recommend it to fans of allegorical works like *The Pilgrim's Progress* or *Hinds' Feet on High Places*, as well as to anyone wrestling with themes of reconciliation, grace, and the cost of true unity.

Rating: 5 stars

# What Readers Are Saying About The Broken Bridge

## EARLY READER REVIEWS AND TESTIMONIALS

"*The Broken Bridge is a tremendous read! You will be caught up from the first word and carried along as if you are part of the story, not able to extricate yourself from the experience, but quite content to continue being swept along as you live this fantastic experience! Truly, it is the best Christian fiction book I have read since Hinds Feet on High Places, and I actually find the pace and excitement to be much greater in The Broken Bridge!*"— Brenda R. Miller

"*I thoroughly enjoyed this beautiful Christian novel, The Broken Bridge. The first page drew me in, and I was drawn to the book naturally each day. I am pleased to write that just as a mystery novel keeps me captivated, so did your book have a subtle essence of a good mystery. I was anxious to learn the savior of these people who suffered so terribly, as sin has brought to mankind in his fall. Your characters were interesting and complete. I suffered with your characters, I hoped with your characters, and I rejoiced with them.*"— Olivia Snead

"*Cleveland writes loss in a way that made my chest ache. Even so, there's a steady thread of hope woven in, even through the darker passages, that kept me turning pages long after midnight.*" –5 Star Editorial Review, Literary Titan

# *Acknowledgments*

## WITH DEEP GRATITUDE

This book would not exist without the extraordinary support, dedication, and expertise of several remarkable individuals who believed in this story and helped bring it to life.

**Elizabeth Mackey** deserves tremendous recognition for her artistic vision and creative genius in crafting the perfect cover design. Her ability to capture the essence of the story in a single image is truly remarkable, and I couldn't have asked for a more talented designer to represent this work.

To my early readers—**Brenda Miller**, **Olivia Snead**, and **Shannon Pettenger**—thank you for your invaluable insights and unwavering commitment to helping shape this story. Your careful attention to plot development, character arcs, and narrative flow, along with your thoughtful editing suggestions, transformed this manuscript in ways I never could have achieved alone. Your feedback was both honest and encouraging, pushing me to dig deeper and write better.

**Jennifer Haskin**, my editor, deserves special recognition for her exceptional dedication to excellence. Jennifer doesn't just edit—she elevates. Her meticulous attention to detail, her keen understanding of storytelling, and her commitment to quality that goes far beyond the call of duty have made this book immeasurably better. Working with her has been both a privilege and an education. If you'd like a great editor, you can reach her at https://frontpageediting.com/

Finally, to my wife, **Jody Cleveland**, who has been my most trusted collaborator throughout this entire journey. The countless hours you spent discussing storylines, dissecting plot points, analyzing characters, and exploring every aspect of this book were invaluable. Your feedback wasn't just helpful—it was transformative. You understood this story as deeply as I did, and your insights shaped it in fundamental ways. Thank you for being my sounding board, my critic, my cheerleader, and my partner in bringing this vision to life.

To all of you, this book is as much yours as it is mine. Thank you for your time, your talent, and your belief in this story.

Cover Design by Elizabeth Mackey at WWW.ElizabethMackeyGraphics.com

# About the Author

## MIKE CLEVELAND

Mike Cleveland brings nearly two decades of pastoral experience to his storytelling, drawing from years of walking alongside people through life's deepest challenges and greatest joys. In 2000, he founded Setting Captives Free Ministries, an international ministry that continues to serve people around the world.

Mike has been married to his wife Jody since 1998, and together they have been blessed with seven children—five here on earth and two precious ones in heaven—and are the proud grandparents of four grandchildren.

Through his writing, Mike explores themes of redemption, sacrifice, and the power of love to bridge even the deepest divides. His debut novel, *The Broken Bridge*, is the first book in *The Bridge Trilogy*, where he weaves together allegory and truth to illuminate the Christian gospel in fresh and compelling ways.

When he's not writing, Mike enjoys hiking the trails of the beautiful Pacific Northwest, spending time with his family, and continuing his work with Setting Captives Free Ministries, where he remains committed to sharing hope and freedom with all who need it.

CHAPTER ONE

# The Great Bridge

## WHERE TWO SHORES BECOME ONE

F idel was on a mission to find his bride-to-be. Tomorrow at midday, he and Verita would be wed at the very center of the Great Bridge. But first they needed to discuss final plans with Harmonia, who arranged all the sacred ceremonies and was known throughout both shores as a harmony weaver. That meant crossing the bridge from his home in Eastlight to Westshore, where Verita awaited him.

As he approached the Great Bridge, familiar laughter echoed across the gleaming stone archway. He clutched a small wooden box containing Verita's wedding gift, weaving through the crowd with quiet confidence. Weathered hands from years of tending orchards belied his twenty-two years. His unruly black hair was barely tamed despite his attempts to control it.

The moment he stepped onto the Great Bridge, morning light danced across the stone beneath his feet. Ahead, he could see the central plaza, where intricate mosaic tiles caught the light, and where merchants from both sides of the Vitae River had displayed their wares in a brilliant tapestry of colors. The elders always said that true strength wasn't in stone or steel, but in lives bound tightly together. Fidel felt that truth humming beneath his feet as the bridge vibrated, alive with community.

"Make way for the bridegroom!" called out Abundus, whose fruit stand overflowed with perfect specimens from the eastern orchards. He tossed a ripe pomegranate to Fidel, who caught it one-handed without breaking stride, his deep brown eyes crinkling with an easy smile.

"A gift of fertility for your wedding feast!" Abundus grinned. "They say a good wife is one of life's rarest treasures; don't lose her."

Fidel's ears reddened as nearby shoppers applauded and offered their blessings.

A few steps ahead, an elderly man from Westshore struggled with a heavy crate of pottery. Without hesitation, a young man from Eastlight helped lift one end. As they carried it together toward the western side, the youth asked earnest questions about the glazing technique, and the elder's weathered face lit up as he shared his knowledge.

The bridge vibrated slightly beneath them, not from weakness, but from the rhythm of hundreds of feet moving in unity. It was said in both towns that nothing pleased the Creator more than neighbors living in peace. The Great Bridge was a marvel—so vast it would take a man a full half-hour to walk from shore to shore at a steady pace. Designed for far more than mere crossing, it was the hub for culture and community, for trade, and for teaching the young.

"Is that gift for Verita?" called Clementia, the elderly weaver whose nimble fingers worked threads of gold and azure into patterns that told stories of the two towns' shared history. "Come now, let an old woman admire it!"

Fidel hesitated, then carefully opened the box to reveal a pendant of polished amber, inside which sat a perfect white flower that bloomed only on the western shore where Verita lived. The crowd leaned in and sighed appreciatively.

"The Eternus bloom," Clementia breathed, her eyes bright with recognition. "It's a symbol of love that never fades."

"They say love like that must be touched by the Creator," added Sapientia, granddaughter of the bridge's chief architect, her voice filled with reverence.

Fidel nodded. "She deserves something that won't wither. Nothing less."

He closed the box and tucked it securely into his vest pocket. His gaze drifted westward, where the bridge stretched across the river toward the place his beloved awaited.

As Fidel continued westward, laughter drew his attention to children playing on one of the wide promenades. A girl with the distinctive braided hair of Westshore clapped her hands in rhythm while a boy in the earth-toned tunic of Eastlight tried to match her pattern. When he stumbled over the sequence, she patiently started again, their different accents blending into shared giggles.

Nearby, two scholars debated in friendly conversation. "But surely the eastern method of crop rotation yields better results in sandy soil," one argued. The other nodded thoughtfully. "Perhaps. Yet our western terracing prevents erosion. What if we combined them?"

The ancient architects had designed this Great Bridge not merely as a crossing, but as a living heart where two communities could become one. People often marveled at the structure's beauty, but Fidel knew the true wonder wasn't the bridge itself; rather, it was the unity it provided. The old proverb etched on the cornerstone came to his mind: *In the eyes of the Maker, no one is foreign; only family not yet met.*

As Fidel continued his walk, he noticed a young woman—slight, pale, eyes cast downward—standing half-hidden behind the weaver's stall. Her fingers fidgeted with a loose thread at her sleeve, and when an elder greeted her kindly, she only nodded and stepped farther back.

"Timidia, the weaver's daughter," Sapientia murmured quietly to Fidel. "Poor child can barely speak above a whisper. Sweet soul, but always afraid of being seen."

Fidel nodded, moved by the contrast. In a community so full of laughter and light, Timidia seemed like a shadow cast by something unseen.

As the sun approached its zenith, Fidel saw the communal kitchen bustling with activity. A young mother approached with empty hands, worry creasing her brow. Before she could even speak, an elderly baker pressed a warm loaf into her arms and quietly slipped dried fruit into her basket. No one tallied their share or kept a silent score. In this place, giving was its own reward.

Benigna chopped vegetables from her eastern gardens while singing harmonies with Concordia, who kneaded dough made from western wheat. The Creator, they believed, had blessed each shore with unique gifts; not so they would boast, but so they would bless.

"Will Verita join us for the midday meal?" asked Benevolus, the elder whose name matched his kind nature.

"She's meeting with the ceremony attendants at Harmonia's studio," Fidel replied. "Harmonia herself is designing our ceremony."

"A fitting choice," Benevolus nodded. "Is it not Harmonia who weaves harmony between hearts, creating ceremonies that unite souls as surely as the bridge unites shores?"

As if summoned by their conversation, Fidel spotted Harmonia herself approaching, her ceremonial sash flowing with each graceful step. Her eyes, sharp with precision, softened when she smiled.

"Fidel, I was hoping to find you," she called out.

"And I was just looking for you," replied Fidel. "Do you know where I might find my bride-to-be? We were wanting to discuss final plans for the wedding with you."

"Verita is in my studio. She has shared the most wonderful ideas for your ceremony. The symbolism of joining hands at the exact center point—where east meets west in perfect balance—it's inspired!"

Fidel smiled, thinking of his beloved. "Trust Verita to see the deeper meaning in the ancient design of the bridge."

"The bridge merely reflects what was always intended between your hearts," she replied. "Two sides, one foundation. That's how the bridge stands. That's how love endures."

"Come," she said, motioning toward her studio, "Verita waits, and there are decisions about tomorrow that require both bride and bridegroom."

As they crossed onto the western shore and approached Harmonia's studio, Fidel paused at the threshold, his hand frozen on the door handle as his breath caught in his throat.

Inside, Verita stood examining architectural drawings spread across a broad table, her profile illuminated by golden light streaming through tall windows. She moved with unconscious grace, her fingers tracing the elegant lines of the bridge's design with the same reverence she might show a sacred text.

For a moment, Fidel forgot how to breathe. At nineteen, she was radiant—not just beautiful, but luminous, as though the Creator had poured extra light into her very being.

Harmonia, sensing the quiet weight of the moment, offered Fidel a warm smile. "I'll be in the archive room," she whispered. "Take your time." She stepped through a side doorway, leaving Fidel alone in the golden-lit stillness.

Verita looked up, sensing Fidel's presence, and their eyes locked across the room. Time seemed to suspend itself.

"Fidel," she whispered, his name falling from her lips like a prayer. The truth of her nature shone in her gaze—straightforward, unwavering, pure—but now he saw something more. Wonder. The same breathless amazement that had stolen his voice.

He stepped toward her, still speechless. Her eyes never left his, and he could see his own awe reflected there.

"You're..." he began, then stopped, shaking his head with a soft laugh. "How do you do that?"

"Do what?" she asked, though her voice was barely above a whisper.

"Make me forget every word I've ever learned," he said. "Make me feel like I'm seeing the sun rise for the first time."

A blush bloomed across her cheeks, but she didn't look away. Instead, she moved toward him with that same unconscious grace.

"And you," she said, reaching up to touch his face with trembling fingers, "make me understand why the poets write about love as if it were something alive, something that could steal your breath and give it back transformed."

Verita moved into Fidel's embrace, and for a moment, neither spoke; their embrace said more than words. They simply existed together in the warmth of love.

"I visited the Hall of Records today," Verita said at last. Uncle Aldric had always encouraged her scholarly pursuits—wisdom that had guided her since he took her in as an orphaned child. "I found something remarkable in the ancient texts."

She led him to a scroll carefully unfurled on a side table. "Look at this inscription from the original bridge drawings."

Fidel's eyes widened as he read: *When division threatens to separate what belongs together, remember this bridge. What love joins, nothing can divide.*

"Our wedding tomorrow," Verita whispered, "will be another thread in the tapestry that began long ago."

Fidel slid his hand into his pocket and gently touched the wooden box containing the amber pendant, suddenly certain that their union was somehow part of a larger design.

"Let's take a walk to the spot where tomorrow we become husband and wife," Fidel said, after they had spoken with Harmonia about last-minute wedding plans.

The afternoon had grown long as they made their way from Harmonia's studio, and evening shadows began to stretch across the bridge. Her chestnut hair caught the fading light, weaving threads of copper and gold through the loose curls that framed her face. Nothing false ever crossed her lips. Her name, Verita, wasn't just a title, it was the essence of who she was.

When she was eight, Verita had watched her beloved grandfather promise to return from a trading journey "before the harvest moon." She waited at their garden gate every evening, but he never came home—he had started a new family in a distant village. That night, through her tears, young Verita made a vow: she would never leave anyone waiting on a lie.

"Tomorrow feels too distant," she said, her fingers interlacing with his.

Fidel nodded, studying the firm line of her jaw. His own broad shoulders relaxed in her presence, the constant vigilance he maintained as guardian of the eastern orchards unnecessary when they were together.

Fidel had learned about vigilance early. His father, Gamiel, had been full of grand promises but had courted half the village behind his mother's back. When Fidel was twelve, his father simply disappeared, leaving only a note about "needing freedom." Young Fidel had made his own silent promise: whatever else he became, he would not be a man who broke faith.

"The stars will refuse to set tonight," he agreed, drawing her closer.

They paused at the exact center of the bridge as the sun set and the first stars appeared. Beneath them, the Vitae River shimmered nearly a hundred feet below, its surface catching the evening stars like scattered coins. Neither seemed able to release the other's hand.

"I should return home, it's getting dark," Verita whispered, though she made no move to leave. "My family has prepared the ceremonial garments."

"And my father expects me for the blessing meal," Fidel replied, equally motionless.

Verita's eyes searched his face in the fading light. "Sometimes I try to imagine what my life would have been without you," she said softly, "and I can't. It's like trying to imagine the bridge without its keystone."

When she finally stepped back, the space between them seemed to protest the separation.

"Until tomorrow," Verita promised. "When we meet again, it will be to never part."

"Signal me like usual when you get home," Fidel said.

Verita nodded, then stepped to the edge of the bridge where she kept her lantern. "Always."

They each turned toward their own distant shore. From his vantage point, Fidel could still see both shores at once, their entire world held together by this singular bridge. Tomorrow, they would be joined—just as surely, just as beautifully—as the two shores were bound by stone and sacred design.

When Fidel arrived home, he scanned across the river. Soon, a gentle arc of light swept across the darkness from her shore—the signal for "safe." Then came their practiced sequence: a loop and two brief flashes meaning "home well," followed by the familiar curve that meant "love."

He raised his own lantern in response: a quick zigzag for "glad," then their special signal—a slow figure eight meaning "forever bound," and finally the arc for "love."

From across the water, her reply came: three brief pulses for "tomorrow," a triangle for "joy," and the double curve for "always."

Their rich communication had begun when Verita's uncle Aldric taught her the traditional signals used by bridge watchmen. During their courtship, she had taught many of these patterns to Fidel, creating a language only they shared.

As their final signals faded into the night, a strange stillness settled over the valley. The ever-present chorus of night birds fell silent. Even the gentle lapping of the river against the bridge's foundations seemed to hush, as if the very earth were holding its breath.

# CHAPTER TWO

# When The Earth Shook

## FOUNDATIONS UNDONE

T he first tremor struck mid-morning, as Fidel and his parents were preparing to leave for the wedding ceremony on the bridge. His mother screamed. His father tried to shelter her. Fidel dropped to his knees. Something had changed in the world. The air itself seemed to congeal, pressing against his skin with unnatural heaviness. A metallic taste coated his tongue, and his ears popped as if he'd descended rapidly from a great height.

The familiar scents of their home, the cedar shelves and stone floors, were suddenly overlaid with something acrid and foreign, like sulfur rising from deep beneath the earth. Even before the ground began to move, Fidel's body recognized the wrongness: every hair standing on end, his stomach hollowing with instinctive dread. He felt it before he heard it, before the ground began to shudder beneath his home.

Then came the noise; a deep, guttural groan from far below the earth, as if the foundations of the world itself were shifting. The sound vibrated through his bones before reaching his ears, a primordial bass note that seemed to liquefy his insides and turn his legs to water. Objects crashed from shelves; walls cracked as if lines drawn by an invisible hand.

"Creator save us," his mother gasped from the doorway ... her face pale from fear.

Fidel stumbled outside. He could see the bridge in the distance, shaking, swaying and starting to crumble.

The second tremor came stronger than the first, and with it came a strange, crawling darkness that seemed to flow over the stones. Dust billowed upward, catching in his throat and stinging his eyes. The crawling darkness moved unlike natural shadow; it seemed to drink the light, spreading like spilled ink across surfaces it touched, leaving behind a residue that dulled the once-vibrant colors of the mosaic tiles.

The air filled with a cacophony of sounds: the high-pitched whine of stone grinding against stone, the percussive crack of splitting wood, the desperate screams that seemed to come from everywhere at once, and beneath it all, that continuous, terrible groaning from the earth itself.

The third tremor ripped a jagged scar across the heavens. For a terrible instant, the bridge stood frozen in the gash of unnatural light, its graceful arc suspended in broken fragments. Then the center collapsed, stones tumbling into the suddenly violent waters below.

The Vitae River, which just that morning had carried gentle merchant vessels and laughing children, now raged with unnatural fury. Where peaceful passenger barges had just ferried families between shores, treacherous whirlpools now swirled with deadly force. The calm current that had welcomed all travelers was gone, replaced by churning rapids that devoured everything they touched. No boat could survive such waters; no soul could cross what had become a liquid barrier as impassable as any mountain.

With the chaos came something else, a feeling Fidel had never experienced before. A tightness in his chest. A desperate fear. A voice inside him that whispered, *Save yourself first.*

\*\*\*

As the dust began to settle, the morning light revealed a world forever changed; not just by physical destruction, but by an invisible poison that had entered creation itself, breaking something fundamental within human hearts. It became clear that the terrible tragedy went far beyond a crumbling bridge and a raging river; the crumbling and raging had entered the human heart and behavior.

\*\*\*

Midday revealed the full horror of what had happened. A cloying mist hovered over the churning waters, thick with the dust of pulverized stone. The stench of wet debris, disturbed riverbed, and something else, something coppery and primal, hung in the air. Birds that normally sang remained eerily silent, as if even they understood that something fundamental had been broken.

The only sounds were human weeping and shouting, punctuated by the hollow, rhythmic thudding of debris still occasionally breaking free to fall into the river below. Each impact added to the churning of the water; a visual echo of how their world would become turbulent, chaotic. The bridge's once-graceful arc was now a jagged wound across the sky. Bodies floated face down in the churning waters; men, women, and children who had been crossing when the center gave way.

"Elinor! ELINOR!" A man pointed to the body of a young woman on the rocks below. "My daughter ... she was delivering bread to the west side..." Two others pulled him back from the edge of the broken bridge as he sobbed.

His cries joined the chorus of anguish that rose from both shores. Merchants dropped their crates and fell to their knees, staring across the river in disbelief. A husband called out a name that echoed unanswered across the divide.

Near the eastern shore, a woman knelt over the broken body of her husband, pulled from the wreckage that had washed up on the bank. "We were married for sixty-three years," she cried to no one in particular, stroking his still face. "Not once did we speak harshly to each other. Not once." Her tears fell onto his cold cheeks. "What will I do now? What will I do without you?"

Yet even as grief consumed them, something darker began to stir. The earthquake had not only cracked stone and timber—it had fractured something within human hearts themselves.

On the west side, a man sprinted toward the edge of a massive sinkhole, clutching a coil of rope, his eyes locked on his wife, who clung to a crumbling beam lodged deep in the rubble below. "Hold on, Marta!" he called, bracing to lower the rope.

Before he could drop it down, another man yanked the coil from his hands. "No—I need this! My son's trapped down there!" He pointed to a small figure wedged beneath broken concrete just yards away. "Give it back!" the first man shouted, lunging for the rope. "She was first! Marta was first!"

They wrestled for the rope, both men's faces contorted with a desperation that bordered on savagery—a look unthinkable in their peaceful community just hours earlier.

While they fought, the woman lost her grip and vanished into the darkness below, and the boy's faint cries were silenced beneath shifting rubble.

As the immediate shock began to fade, something deeper started to crack within them. Where once every need was met with open hands, now eyes narrowed in calculation. A woman turned her back on a weeping stranger. Two men argued over who had the right to scarce supplies. A merchant, watching the disaster unfold, quietly raised his prices—not out of need, but opportunity. If others would suffer, he reasoned, he might as well profit. This was no mere collapse of stone—it was the beginning of distrust, division, and self-preservation.

Elder Pax moved among the grieving, his weathered face drawn with confusion as much as sorrow. "Before today, we knew nothing of fear, nothing of division, nothing of self-preservation," he murmured. "How could such perfect harmony shatter so completely?"

He paused, watching the churning waters with ancient eyes. "My grandmother spoke of old legends," he said to those gathered near. "She said the Vitae River rages when the heart of the land is broken, and will not calm until it is mended by a great sacrifice of love." He shook his head slowly. "I thought them merely stories to frighten children into kindness."

Fidel moved through the chaos in a daze, one thought pounding in his mind: Verita. Had she been crossing already? Was she among the bodies in the water? Or buried under rubble? Or was she on the western shore, as unreachable as if she had passed beyond life itself?

Fidel and his parents returned home, thankful to be alive, but terrified to find out who wasn't. They began to sift through what was left of their home. As he stepped over shattered beams and broken tiles, something caught the light, a glint half-buried beneath a pile of broken stone. He knelt and brushed it free with trembling hands. It was the wooden box.

The hinges were bent, the surface scratched, but when he pried it open, the pendant lay unharmed inside. The amber caught the morning light, and the Eternus bloom, impossibly, still shone white and perfect, unharmed by the disaster.

Fidel's breath caught. In a world unmade, here was proof that something had endured. Love. Truth. The promises they made. Whatever else had fallen, this had not.

He pressed the pendant to his heart. "You're alive," he whispered. "You have to be."

***

The gap between the shores seemed to widen with each passing moment. The opposite bank, once so familiar it felt like an extension of home, now appeared as distant and foreign as the far side of the moon. Children born after would never understand what was lost; the perfect harmony, the natural unity, the effortless communion that had defined life before the catastrophe.

"All my children were on the west side visiting their aunt, uncle and cousins," a gray-haired woman sobbed into her hands. "All four of them. Now I cannot reach them. I cannot even know if they live."

Harmonia worked tirelessly, directing efforts to comfort the grieving and organize memorial services for the fallen. But even her gentle wisdom could find no words for such destruction. "It's as if something has entered the very hearts of the people," she murmured, watching neighbors argue over scarce supplies. "Some corruption I cannot name."

As the day went on, the true scale of the catastrophe was revealed; not just the bridge, but buildings in both communities had collapsed. Landmarks were destroyed. The perfect order of their world had shattered in an instant, leaving chaos in its place. The physical chasm in the bridge was merely the visible manifestation of a deeper rupture—one that had opened within human hearts, creating for the first time the terrible possibility of choosing self over community.

"Verita!" Fidel's voice grew hoarse as he called across the impossible gap. "Verita!"

Only his echo answered, mocking his desperation.

His agony and despair drove him to the ruined eastern edge, eyes straining for any glimpse of her on the far shore. The ache in his chest had become a sharp physical pain; a hollowness that threatened to consume him from within. They had never been separated before, not like this. The absence of her felt like the absence of his own heartbeat.

"Have you seen a young woman with chestnut hair? Her name is Verita." He asked everyone he passed, his words increasingly desperate. "She was to be my bride today."

Some shook their heads sadly. Others were too lost in their own grief to answer.

As twilight approached, Fidel made his way to the eastern shore, to the highest point where he could look across the widened river to the western shore, now lit by countless fires and torches. Were they mourning there as well? Did they have their own memorials, their own missing? Was Verita among those lighting lanterns, searching for him as desperately as he searched for her?

Fidel sank to his knees, overcome. His prayers to the Creator, once flowing naturally as breath, now churned like a raging river in his mind. The Creator seemed suddenly distant, as if the earthquake had widened not just the physical gap across the river, but some spiritual chasm in humanity as well.

In place of prayer rose something new and terrible; doubt, anger. Had the Creator abandoned them? Had the bridge fallen because of some cosmic punishment? Or worse, had their perfect world been merely an illusion all along, now stripped away to reveal a harsher truth beneath?

Yet something in Fidel resisted. The meaning of his name, Faithful, had never felt more like a challenge than it did now. Faithful to what? To whom? To Verita, certainly. But also to something larger, something that the fallen bridge had once embodied but had not created; a unity that existed before the first stone was laid.

Fidel rose to his feet, took a torch from its holder, and began to wave it in the patterns Verita had taught him. Not random gestures of desperation, but the deliberate signals from Uncle Aldric's Night Watchmen's Code. A slow arc—the signal for "safe." A pause. Then another arc, this one traced with trembling hands—"love."

Nothing. The western shore remained silent, giving no sign that anyone had seen his desperate message.

He tried again, this time with the double curve for "always"—their most sacred signal. Again, nothing. The vast distance mocked his efforts, swallowing his light as completely as the earthquake had swallowed their world.

Yet something in Fidel refused to surrender. Whether Verita lived or had perished in the collapse, whether she could see his signals or had drowned in the raging river, he would continue sending his message into the darkness.

As the night deepened, Fidel realized that this flickering conversation with emptiness might become his only connection to hope itself. If she lived, someday she might see. If she didn't...at least the darkness would know he had not stopped calling her name.

The night wind shifted, carrying with it terrible sounds: fragments of weeping, the crash of structures still collapsing. Beneath it all ran the river, once a gentle presence at the heart of their joined communities, now a violent barrier that seemed determined to forever keep apart what belonged together.

# CHAPTER THREE

# Across The Divide

## SIGNALS THROUGH DARKNESS

T he morning of the second day arrived with no mercy, casting a harsh light on a reality Fidel had hoped might prove to be merely a nightmare. The death toll had already risen to seventy-eight confirmed, with dozens still missing.

All night he had maintained his vigil on the eastern shore, torch in hand, sending signal after signal into the darkness using Uncle Aldric's Night Watchmen's Code. A slow arc for "safe." Another arc for "love." The double curve for "always." Each pattern traced with desperate precision, each one swallowed by the vast distance and churning mist.

Nobody had answered. The western shore remained as silent as a tomb.

By first light, his torch was no longer needed, but Fidel's gaze remained fixed on the far shore. If Verita lived, surely she would be watching too. Surely she would see his signals and respond.

Tonight, he told himself. Tonight she'll answer.

***

A small girl sat alone on a pile of rubble when he made his way to the recovery site, clutching a doll made of woven reeds. "My mommy went to get water," she said when Fidel approached. "She told me to wait here. But she's been gone a long time."

Fidel knelt beside her, recognizing her as one of Sapientia's students from the bridge school. "What's your name, little one?"

"Innocentia," she whispered. "Where did the bridge go? When will it come back?"

The simplicity of her question cut through Fidel's heart like a blade. "I don't know," he answered honestly. The old certainty that had guided Fidel's steps was gone, replaced by a fragile hope that felt increasingly desperate.

Within minutes, he spotted an elderly woman who had lost her own home but was helping organize the survivors.

"Cordelia," Fidel called softly. "This is Innocentia. Her mother went for water and hasn't returned."

Cordelia's weathered face immediately softened. "Oh, sweet child. Come, let's get you somewhere safe while we search." She gathered the girl gently. "I'll take her to the women's shelter we've set up. We have other children there, and I'll make sure word spreads about her mother."

"We found another group," said Benevolus, approaching, his once-kindly face now haggard with exhaustion. "Trapped in a section of the lower arcade that had collapsed. Three alive. Five..." He didn't need to finish.

Throughout the morning, Fidel joined different recovery teams, partly to help, partly to continue his search for any sign of Verita. Each body they uncovered brought the same terrible mixture of fear, relief, shame; fear that it might be her, relief when it wasn't, followed immediately by shame at his relief.

A team of rescuers staggered past them, shoulders sagging under the dead weight of a body covered with a cloak. A woman's hand hung limply from beneath the covering, a silver bracelet still glinting on her wrist. Fidel's heart stopped; Verita had worn such a bracelet. He rushed forward, his hands already trembling as he reached for the cloak's edge.

His hands shook so violently he couldn't release the fabric, bile burning his throat as relief and shame crashed through him simultaneously. It wasn't her. Someone else's loss. Someone else's devastation while he stood grateful over a stranger's corpse.

"Twenty-six recovered so far," said Pax, the community elder, his weathered face drawn with grief. "Many more are still missing."

***

The second night, Fidel returned to the shore with renewed determination. He lit his torch and began the sequence again, more deliberately this time. First, the arc for "safe"—letting her know he had survived. Then "love"—the message that mattered most. Then "always"—their sacred promise.

He waited, torch held steady, eyes straining across the water.

Nothing.

He tried again, this time adding new signals from the Night Watchmen's Code. "Here." "Alive." "Waiting." Each gesture precise, each pause measured.

Still nothing.

The western shore remained dark, offering no answering light, no sign that anyone had seen his desperate messages.

***

By the end of the first week, a grim routine had established itself. During the day, Fidel worked with the recovery teams, searching through rubble, helping to bury the dead, comforting the grieving. But as each sunset approached, he found himself drawn back to the shore with an urgency that bordered on compulsion.

Night after night, he stood at the water's edge, torch in hand, tracing the same patterns. Night after night, the darkness swallowed his signals without response.

The community was beginning to fracture. Neighbors hoarded their remaining food. Children scavenged like wild animals through the rubble. Families turned on each other over scraps of shelter. The bridge had connected more than shores—it had connected hearts. Without it, something essential in their nature was breaking down.

"There's something strange about this destruction," said Elder Pax, examining a fragment of stone closely during one of their planning meetings. "I've walked across this bridge every day for forty years. Its structure was perfect; it should have withstood any natural tremor. But this..." He pointed to a dark discoloration that ran through the stone like a vein. "This is something I've never seen before. It's as if something corrupted it from within."

***

On the eighth night, Fidel's hands trembled as he lit his torch. A terrible thought had begun to take root: What if she couldn't respond because she was dead?

He forced himself to signal anyway. "Safe." "Love." "Always." But for the first time, the gestures felt hollow, mechanical. He was signaling to empty air, to a memory, to hope that grew thinner with each passing night.

A cry went up from the water's edge that morning. A boat—Willful Venture—was being prepared; Captain Power at the helm; the first to attempt the crossing since the earthquake.

"Look at those waters," one of the rowers said, his face pale as he watched the churning current. "It's like the river itself has gone mad."

"The boat will be torn apart," another protested, gripping his oar with white knuckles. "Those aren't natural rapids anymore—they're a death trap."

Captain Power's jaw was set with grim determination. "My wife and children are on that shore. I'll not leave them stranded."

"We could wait," suggested a third rower. "Perhaps the waters will calm—"

"They've been raging for over a week," Power cut him off. "How long do we wait while families starve? While children cry for parents they cannot reach?" He looked each man in the eye. "I'm going. Any who wish to stay behind may do so."

Despite their fear, all six rowers took their positions. Whatever terror the river held, the thought of their loved ones trapped on the far shore was worse.

Six strong rowers fought against the still-turbulent current, muscles straining as they drove the vessel toward the western shore, determined to bridge the gap.

Everyone stopped to watch, hope rising. Perhaps this was the beginning of reconnection.

Willful Venture made it less than halfway across before a sudden surge caught it broadside. In an instant, the boat capsized. The crowd gasped in collective horror as all six disappeared beneath the churning waters.

Three surfaced, struggling. One managed to grab floating debris and was eventually pulled back to the eastern shore. The other two were swept downstream, their fate unknown. The remaining three never resurfaced at all.

The hope that had briefly flared died just as quickly. An old man shook his head. "Strength and willpower can't span what's broken," he murmured. "Not anymore."

\*\*\*

The first burials began; rows of fresh graves on a hillside overlooking the broken bridge. Fidel stood at the back as a mother and father lowered their young son, Avel, into the earth. The boy had been found crushed beneath a fallen column, his hand clutching a letter. His twin brother sat watching, completely still.

"He was only on the bridge because I sent him with a message," the father gasped, his voice hollow with guilt. "If I had gone myself..."

As dirt fell on Avel's shrouded body, his twin brother suddenly erupted from his silence. "Where was the creator?" he screamed, his child's voice cracking with rage. "Where was he when the stones fell?"

The memorial dissolved into chaos of grief and fury. Fidel felt the boy's anguish like a physical blow. Where indeed was the Creator? Had He abandoned them? Was this punishment for some unknown sin?

***

On the tenth night, Fidel's signals grew more erratic. His usual precise patterns gave way to desperate improvisation. He tried every signal from the Night Watchman's Code that Uncle Aldric had taught Verita. "Help." "Danger." "Come home." "Still here."

The darkness consumed them all without response.

He began to signal random patterns, hoping that if she lived but couldn't remember the proper codes, she might at least see the movement and know he was trying to reach her. He waved the torch in great sweeping arcs, held it steady for long moments, created spirals and zigzags and every shape he could imagine.

Nothing.

***

By the twelfth night, doubt had crystallized into a cold certainty that sat in his chest like a stone. She was gone. Dead in the collapse, drowned in the river, buried beneath tons of rubble. He was signaling to no one, talking to emptiness, clinging to hope that had died with the bridge.

Still, he came to the shore. Not from hope now, but from habit. From the inability to stop. From love that had nowhere to go but into the darkness.

"Safe," he signaled, though she would never be safe again. "Love," though love felt like mockery. "Always," though always had been severed by catastrophe.

The torch felt impossibly heavy in his hands.

***

Unitas found him there on the thirteenth night, slumped at the water's edge, the torch burned down to a stub beside him.

"You should rest," Unitas said gently, settling beside him on the rocky shore. "You've been at this for nearly two weeks."

"She's dead," Fidel said, the words coming out flat and lifeless. "I've been signaling to no one."

"You don't know that."

"Seventy-eight confirmed dead. Dozens still missing. No response to any signal for thirteen nights." Fidel's voice cracked. "She's gone, Unitas. And I...I don't know how to stop."

Unitas placed a hand on his shoulder. "Love doesn't stop because the beloved might be gone. It continues because that's what love does."

"What's the point?" Fidel demanded, anger flaring suddenly. "What's the point of love that can't reach its object? What's the point of faithfulness to someone who may not exist anymore?"

Unitas was quiet for a long moment. "Perhaps," he said finally, "the point isn't whether she receives your signals. Perhaps the point is that you send them. That love persists even in the face of silence." Unitas' had a gift for simply being present, listening and caring.

***

On the fourteenth night, Fidel almost didn't come to the shore. The ritual had become torture, each unanswered signal another blow to his dwindling hope. But as darkness fell, he found his feet carrying him to the familiar spot, torch in hand.

Maybe this would be the last time. Maybe tomorrow he would begin the long work of accepting that she was gone, of learning to live with half a heart, of finding some way to exist in a world where the bridge would never be rebuilt.

For the first time in two weeks, Fidel truly looked around him. His own desperation had blinded him to the quiet surrenders happening everywhere. A woman who had called across the divide every morning for her children now sat silent on her doorstep, staring at nothing. A husband who had shouted himself hoarse searching for his wife now walked the streets like a ghost, his voice reduced to whispers. Grandparents, who had built their lives around visiting family across the river, now sat with hands folded, their eyes no longer seeking the far shore but fixed on the ground before them.

They had all stopped hoping. They had all accepted the unacceptable. Perhaps it was time for him to join them in their grim peace.

He lit the torch with trembling hands. The flame seemed dimmer tonight, or perhaps his eyes were too blurred with tears to see it clearly.

"Safe," he signaled one last time, the gesture barely visible through his shaking.

"Love."

"Always."

Then he lowered the torch and prepared to turn away, to walk back to his empty home and his half-life of mere survival.

A sound came from behind him—footsteps on the path. Fidel turned, startled out of his despair, and stepped back from the water's edge. A figure was approaching along the path that led to the village, moving with confident strides. In the shifting moonlight, Fidel could make out measuring tools hanging from their belt, and a medallion stamped with scales of justice glinting at their neck.

Whoever it was, they carried themselves with the assurance of one who had authority.

# CHAPTER FOUR

# Regulus

## THE LAW-MAKER

T he next morning, crowds gathered to meet the stranger, who had come into town the night before. He walked toward them, his back straight as a plumb line, carrying measuring instruments—rulers, squares, compasses—and wore a medallion stamped with scales of justice.

"I am Regulus," he announced, his voice carrying authority. "I am the Master Builder, and I have come down from my home on Mt. Covenantus to help you. Let's get to work and get that bridge rebuilt!"

The people stirred with hope. After two weeks of watching Fidel's nightly vigil at the river's edge, signaling across the darkness to silence that never answered, finally someone had arrived who promised action.

Fidel had largely abandoned his desperate signaling ritual—now only attempting signals once or twice a week, using a lantern, convinced it was useless but unable to stop entirely. Those occasional signals had become hollow gestures rather than hope. He would whisper her name to the darkness, sometimes singing their betrothal song to the wind, but his heart had begun to accept what his mind refused to acknowledge: Verita was likely gone forever.

And while Fidel and the rest of the village was beginning to despair, Regulus offered what seemed like salvation.

***

One evening in late spring, Regulus strode toward the windswept shore where Fidel stood, lantern in hand—one of his infrequent attempts at signaling beneath the darkening sky.

"Put that down," he commanded. "Your signals solve nothing. What you need is to build the bridge—and build it using proper order, perfect measurements, and strict adherence to the code."

Fidel lowered the lantern slowly, his eyes red-rimmed but suddenly bright with fragile hope. "Can you rebuild the bridge? Can you help us reach the other side?"

"I can show you the way," Regulus said, unfurling blueprints of exquisite detail. "But everyone must follow my instructions exactly. There can be no deviation, no error, no imperfection."

Something cold twisted in Fidel's stomach. The absolute certainty in Regulus's voice, the way he dismissed any possibility of failure—it reminded him of another man who had been so sure of himself. His biological father had spoken with the same confident authority when making promises he never intended to keep.

But this was different, Fidel told himself. Regulus was offering something real, something built on law and order, not empty words. Wasn't this exactly what his father had lacked—genuine commitment to standards? Fidel pushed down his unease. He had to believe this would work.

***

As early summer heat began to build, Fidel helped prepare the construction site. He discovered Regulus alone one evening, staring at a small, worn book bound in leather. The master builder's hands—usually so steady with his measuring tools—trembled slightly as he traced a diagram within.

"Is that from your training on Mt. Covenantus?" Fidel asked gently.

Regulus startled, then quickly composed his features. "Yes. My father's Scroll of Perfection."

His finger paused on a page showing a child's architectural model.

"I was seven when I built my first bridge," he said. "Spent weeks carving each timber, sanding every joint smooth as silk. When I presented it... Father held it to the light, found one angle off by a hair's width. 'Rubbish,' he said—and swept it into the fire."

Regulus's knuckles whitened around the scroll. "I watched my bridge burn while he explained that 'almost-perfect' was the enemy of excellence."

He straightened his already immaculate clothing. "I will not fail him now. This bridge will be perfect—no matter what it costs."

The villagers gathered around as Regulus drove a golden stake into the ground precisely where the old bridge had begun. "Here," he proclaimed, "we will build a perfect structure. One that cannot fail if you obey my instructions."

Regulus established his headquarters beneath a white canvas tent. From there, he began assessing each villager according to his strict code.

Many failed to qualify.

"Your hands are too calloused," he told one worker. "Your back is crooked."

At the slightest imperfection, Regulus dismissed not just individuals—but entire teams.

He turned to Alma, a grandmother who had raised seven children and built half the village's hearths.

"Your hands shake too much," he said flatly. "The law of the bridge is absolute," Regulus declared, oblivious to the wounds his words inflicted. "It cannot bend to accommodate weakness."

And it didn't—but the community did, fracturing under the pressure of impossible standards.

Soon, those who remained couldn't bear to look at those who'd been dismissed. Shame and survivor's guilt built invisible walls between families, between friends who had once shared everything. The village fractured—split not by stone, but by new and brutal lines of supposed worthiness that had never existed before.

\*\*\*

Six weeks into Regulus's work, as the summer sun blazed overhead, the bridge foundation began to take shape with impressive speed. The stonework was solid, the engineering sound, and for the first time in months, genuine hope flickered in the community.

That evening, Fidel made one of his rare trips to the shore. The twice-weekly ritual had become more habit than hope, but something compelled him to try once more. He raised his lantern and traced the familiar arc—

"Love."

Nothing. As usual.

But then—wait—a light flickered from the western shore. Did he see right? Fidel's heart lurched. He signaled again, hands trembling.

"Safe."

The answering light came clearer this time, mimicking his pattern. But was it really her? It could be anyone holding a lantern, anyone who had seen his signals and was now mocking him with false hope.

Fidel's hands shook as he raised his lantern again. He traced a pattern only Verita would know—three loops in the air, the same motion he had drawn in the sand the day he proposed to her, when he asked her to be his forever.

The distant light hesitated.

Then came the response that stopped his heart—two brief flashes. The Night Watchman's signal for "yes" that Uncle Aldric had taught her. Not a mimicked pattern anyone could copy, but the proper response to his proposal. She was saying yes to him again, across the darkness, just as she had that day in the meadow.

His breath caught in his throat. Still not daring to believe, he sent another test—a quick zigzag followed by a figure eight.

"Miss you." "Remember."

The response came without hesitation: a slow double curve, followed by a gentle arc.

"Always." "Love."

"Verita!" he gasped, his voice barely audible. It was her. It was really her.

Fidel's knees gave out completely. He collapsed onto the rocky shore; the lantern falling beside him as great, wrenching sobs tore from his chest. She was alive. After a month and a half of believing her dead, of signaling into a void that never answered, of slowly dying inside with each silent night—she was alive.

"Creator," he wept, pressing his face to the cold stones, "thank you. Thank you." The words came between gasps, his whole body shaking with the force of emotions too long suppressed. "She's alive. She's still there."

With trembling hands, he retrieved his lantern and raised it again. The signals that followed were simple, halting—both of them seemed shocked by this miraculous reconnection. Her light was weak, uncertain, as if she too had given up hope and was startled to see his response. But they were talking. Across the great divide, they were talking again.

When Fidel returned to the construction site the next morning, he worked with renewed energy. Regulus noticed the change immediately.

"Good," the master builder said approvingly. "You're finally focusing on what matters—the work."

But Fidel's focus wasn't on the work. It was on the bridge as a means to an end. For the first time since the collapse, reaching Verita felt possible again.

***

As autumn arrived, Fidel's communication with Verita had grown slightly more complex. Using basic signals from the Night Watchman's Code that Uncle Aldric had taught her, they could exchange simple words. She signaled

"hurt", then

"delay"—something had injured her, that was the reason for her silence. He responded,

"safe"—thankful she had survived.

Using the Night Watchman's Code, their relationship deepened even across the distance. He would signal simple patterns that reminded her of their courtship—a slow figure eight for "remember," a gentle arc for "love," three brief pulses for "tomorrow." She would respond with her own simple signals, coded in light.

Building continued on the bridge, though seemingly very slow.

As the first snows began to fall, the psychological pressure of Regulus's system began to take its toll. Workers stumbled through their tasks, exhausted and fearful. As the winter deepened, the foundation of the new bridge had taken shape—a marvel of precise stonework and mathematical exactitude. But for every stone laid, another was rejected. For every worker who met Regulus's standard one day, two were dismissed the next for falling short.

Soon the bridge extended a third of the way across the river, perfect angles and flawless geometry cutting through the winter mists.

Behind Regulus, the village had completely fractured—those who could meet the standard and those who could not. Even successful workers lived in constant fear. "The law does not make exceptions," he would say. "Either you measure up, or you don't."

Through the bitter cold, Fidel maintained his nightly signals. Verita's responses remained simple but steady—

"safe," "love," "here"

—basic signals that meant everything to him.

"You see," Regulus told the village elders as they stood upon the extending bridge, their breath visible in the frigid air, "this is how it must be done. Perfect materials, perfect measurements, perfect men. Nothing less will span the river."

But as he spoke, the pressure was building. The workers had been measured so many times, found wanting so often, that their hands shook not just from cold but from exhaustion and fear. The winter work was brutal—stones grew slippery with ice, mortar froze before it could set properly, men's fingers went numb and fumbled measurements.

One February morning, a carpenter, who had been working in low temperatures for days, terrified of being dismissed before spring arrived, placed a support beam while his vision blurred from fatigue and frostbite. He was off by a mere quarter inch.

As the beam settled, the ground beneath his feet shimmered faintly—then slowly bled into a muted blue color, the stone taking on the unmistakable hue of fear. The color crept outward in tendrils, as if the bridge itself had inhaled his anxiety and now exhaled judgment. The bridge was stained. Others noticed and glanced around nervously, but said nothing—speaking up in winter meant certain dismissal and potential starvation.

Then, one by one, they chose silence over truth. Rather than alert a foreman in the deadly cold, they built over the flaw, adjusting their own placements to conceal the original mistake. As they did, a dark black stain began to spread from the same spot—deep and inky, the color of deception. It crawled like spilled ink across the pale stone, entwining with the blue beneath their feet.

The two colors mingled and pulsed, a silent witness to the wrongs committed—fear that silenced, lies that built upon lies. Though the surface of the bridge appeared smooth to the casual eye, its true colors could not be hidden. The bridge remembered.

"Truth-stone," muttered a stonemason, stepping closer to examine the stained sections. He had worked on bridges since before the collapse, and his weathered face showed recognition rather than surprise. "My grandfather told stories about stones like these—quarried from the sacred mountains up north. Said they'd show the true heart of anyone who worked with them." He shook his head grimly, glancing at Regulus in the distance. "The old-timers claimed it would reveal what's hidden in a man's soul, make visible what the heart tries to hide."

The workers had all seen it—and they panicked in the winter wind.

"If Regulus sees this!" one began, unable to finish through chattering teeth.

Another rushed for a tar bucket, its contents barely liquid in the cold. "Quick. Before he gets here."

With trembling, frost-bitten hands, they smeared the thick black substance over the stained stone, covering the glowing veins of blue fear and black deception. The tar dulled the unnatural shimmer, cloaking their guilt in false repair. To any observer, it looked like routine winter weatherproofing. To them, it was desperate concealment.

Moments later, Regulus appeared, walking the length of the span with measured steps, his breath forming clouds in the frigid air. He paused, frowning slightly. "What is this tar?"

One worker wiped his hands on his tunic and offered a strained smile through blue lips. "Just winter weatherproofing, sir."

Regulus nodded slowly, suspicion flickering behind his eyes. "No more unnecessary applications. Perfection yields progress," he declared, moving on, oblivious to the hidden flaw born of human limitation and winter's cruel demands.

The workers exchanged glances of silent dread, their faces haggard from months of impossible standards. They knew they weren't perfect, had made errors, but who would dare admit failure to Regulus in the depths of winter? They had come too far, sacrificed too much, survived too long on the edge of dismissal. So they continued building upon the flawed foundation, hoping against hope the bridge would last until spring.

As the snows melted and spring returned to the valley, the bridge had extended more than halfway across the river—a miraculous feat of engineering and precision that had taken nearly eleven months to achieve. But the cost had been enormous. Three-quarters of the village had been deemed unworthy to participate at some point. The remainder worked with trembling hands, measuring multiple times before making a single cut or placing a single stone.

Regulus watched it all with unwavering eyes, his measuring tools constantly in motion. "See how the perfect standard produces perfect results," he would say, ignoring the exhaustion and terror that hung over the project like the spring mists.

***

The fateful day arrived as spring flowers began to bloom—the day when the bridge would reach its critical middle span. Fidel stood with the remaining workers, his face gaunt from months of sleepless labor, but his eyes still burned with determination. If he could just build far enough, the distance between himself and Verita would finally begin to shrink.

As the final beam of the central support was lifted into place on a warm spring morning, a tremor ran through the exhausted workers. The man guiding it into position flinched, his hands cramping after eleven months of impossible labor. The beam shifted a fraction, aligning with the hidden flaw from the bitter February day.

"Careful!" Regulus barked. "Perfection allows no margin for error!"

The worker straightened the beam as best he could, but the damage was already compounding. Like a whisper passing through the crowd, small imperfections had accumulated throughout the structure over the long months, each born of human limitation, each concealed by fear of Regulus's judgment.

Fidel was the first to feel it—a subtle vibration beneath his feet as he ventured onto the farthest extension. The bridge was now supporting the weight of the remaining workforce, all straining to complete what they hoped would be the final push. He paused, looking toward the distant side where Verita waited—he could see her, barely, a figure on the opposite shore who had become real again through months of patient communication. This first sight of her nearly made him collapse from joy. They were so close to reunion he could almost taste it.

He could see her watching this very moment, her hand pressed to her heart as it was whenever she worried for him. The thought of her waiting, hoping, believing in him after nearly a year of separation, drove him forward despite the growing danger.

"Something's wrong," Fidel said, feeling the strange vibration.

"Nonsense," Regulus replied, consulting his perfect diagrams. "The design is flawless."

But the vibration grew stronger. A low groan emanated from deep within the structure where imperfect human hands had failed to match Regulus's immaculate standard for eleven grueling months. The very perfection of his design had become its fatal flaw—it allowed no flexibility, no accommodation for the inevitable human error that accumulated over time.

A sharp crack split the spring air. The workers froze.

"Everyone off!" shouted an elder, feeling the stone shift beneath his feet.

The workers scrambled toward safety, Fidel leading them to the shore, but Regulus stood motionless, disbelief etched on his face.

"Impossible," he whispered, measuring frantically. "The calculations were perfect."

Another crack—louder this time. The bridge shuddered.

"Regulus!" Fidel shouted from the edge. "Come back! It's collapsing!"

But Regulus couldn't accept failure. After eleven months of perfect standards, perfect measurements, perfect demands—it couldn't end like this. He dropped to his knees, clutching his measuring tools to his chest.

"The standard cannot be wrong," he insisted. "It was the people. Every one of you failed to measure up," he shouted.

The fleeing workers felt their hearts shatter—not just from fear, but from the crushing realization that they had been set up to fail all along. They simply could not meet the requirements of the law of the bridge.

Eleven months of labor. Of measuring themselves against impossible standards. Of believing they were the problem.

Rage bloomed in their chests, even as terror froze their limbs.

Fidel watched his path to Verita crumble, and something inside him broke beyond repair—not hope, but the part of him that had believed faithfulness held meaning. That love could conquer through faithful effort, and would be rewarded. After eleven months of signals growing stronger, of reunion drawing closer—it was all crashing down again.

The bridge gave a final, agonizing groan. The section where Regulus knelt tore away from the rest.

For a breathless instant, he hung suspended over the abyss—and in that moment, his father's voice finally fell silent.

*I became you, he realized with horror. I became the man who burns bridges.*

Then he was gone, plummeting into the mists below—still clutching his perfect instruments as he fell.

By some miracle, only one life had been lost. Regulus himself, who had refused to abandon his collapsing creation, had been the sole casualty of his own impossible standards. Several workers had been injured in the panicked escape—broken bones, cuts from falling debris—but all had survived. They stood in stunned silence at how close they had all come to sharing Regulus's fate.

\*\*\*

Dawn broke clear and cold over the river. The villagers gathered at the edge, surveying the destruction. Of Regulus's perfect bridge, only scattered fragments remained—eleven months of work reduced to rubble in moments.

Thomas stood among the wreckage, his pregnant wife beside him, their second child due any day. And suddenly—he saw it all with terrible clarity.

"We weren't building a bridge," he said, his voice hollow with recognition. "We were feeding something that devoured us piece by piece—our sweat, our sleep, our dignity, our neighbors."

He looked down at his blistered hands, scarred from eleven months of severe demands. "In trying to prove our worthiness ... we only revealed our unworthiness."

But even as Thomas spoke these words, doubt crept through the crowd like winter fog. Alma stepped forward, her calloused hands no longer hidden in shame, but her voice carried a tremor of confusion.

"He made us compete for scraps of approval," she said softly, "while the proper work—caring for each other—went undone for nearly a year." She paused, looking at the wreckage. "But... but maybe if we had tried harder? Maybe if we had been more careful?"

The question hung in the air like smoke. Around them, dismissed workers and exhausted survivors began to gather, but instead of unity, a terrible uncertainty spread through their ranks.

"I should have measured twice," whispered one of the carpenters, staring at his calloused hands. "Every time. I should have been better."

"Maybe the standard was right," another said, his voice breaking. "Maybe we really aren't good enough."

The crowd split before Fidel's eyes—some nodding in bitter agreement with Thomas, others looking down at their hands in fresh shame. Even in failure, Regulus's poison lingered. Even in death, his judgment lived on.

An older man who had been dismissed in the first month, stood with tears in his eyes. "Eleven months I've wondered what was wrong with me," he said. "Eleven months I've felt... defective."

"You're not defective," Alma said firmly, but her own voice wavered. "None of us are."

"Then why did it fail?" demanded a young woman, whose husband had been injured in the collapse.

The question echoed across the water, unanswered and unanswerable. They stood together for the first time in eleven months, but the wounds ran too deep for immediate healing. They saw it now—how they'd been turned against one another, how nearly a year of their lives had been consumed by the impossible pursuit of perfection.

Fidel stood alone at the very edge, his eyes fixed on the far side, his entire body trembling not with cold but with a trauma that went deeper than broken bones. After eleven months of growing hope, of patient waiting, of believing that faithful effort meant something—they were back where they started.

But it was worse than that. So much worse.

The collapse hadn't just destroyed the bridge. It had shattered something fundamental inside him—the belief that trying mattered. That persistence had value.

"I did everything right," he whispered to the wind, his voice breaking on each word. "Every stone I laid perfectly. Every measurement exact. I gave everything."

He pressed his hands to his chest, where an ache had opened that felt like drowning from the inside. "I believed. I waited. I hoped. I worked. And for what?"

Verita seemed more unreachable now than ever before—not because of the physical distance, but because he could no longer trust that trying to reach her meant anything at all.

"What if..." The thought formed slowly, like poison crystallizing in his mind. "What if faithful effort is just... setting yourself up for a bigger fall?"

He had given Regulus eleven months of his life. Eleven months of believing that if he just worked hard enough, followed the rules closely enough, measured carefully enough—he could earn his way back to her.

And it had all been a lie.

Not just Regulus's lie, but his own. The lie that effort mattered. That persistence paid off. That faithful love could overcome any obstacle if you just tried hard enough.

"Maybe," he said to the empty air, his voice hollow as wind through broken stones, "maybe some things just can't be reached. Maybe some people are just meant to be alone."

The words fell from his lips like shed blood, each one a small death of the faith that had carried him through the darkest nights.

But even as despair threatened to drown him completely, even as his faith in effort and persistence lay shattered at his feet—one thing remained unbroken.

They were still separated. But they were still connected.

"I will find a way to you," he whispered into the mist, the words coming not from faith but from something deeper—a love that existed beyond success or failure, beyond reward or punishment. "Whatever it takes."

He felt as though his heart had broken along with the bridge, but in a strange way, the breaking had revealed something indestructible at its core.

Fidel turned from the river, his face lined with grief but somehow clearer than before.

"Regulus showed us what doesn't work," he said, his voice carrying across the gathered crowd. "Perfect standards bring perfect condemnation when no one can meet them."

The villagers nodded in somber agreement, the weight of their collective failure and loss heavy upon them. In Fidel's voice, they heard not hope exactly, but something harder—the sound of a man who would not give up, no matter how deeply failure broke his heart.

"I don't know what comes next," he continued, his eyes fixed on the distant shore where Verita waited. "I don't know how we'll ever cross this river. But I know this much—we can't let this failure define us. We can't let the demand for perfection, and our own failure, be the last word."

He paused, looking around at the faces of his neighbors—some defiant, some broken, all marked by eleven months of impossible demands.

"We're still here," he said simply. "We're still breathing. We still love the people on the other side." His voice grew stronger. "That has to count for something. That has to be worth something."

The words were just the stubborn refusal of a man to let despair have the final say.

***

The following morning, Fidel found himself drawn back to the wreckage. Garus, the master stonemason, was already there sorting through the rubble.

"Mind if I help?" Fidel asked quietly.

Garus looked up, surprised. "I need to understand why some parts held while others didn't," Fidel explained.

Something in his tone made Garus nod. "See this joint here?" He pointed to where two stones had separated cleanly. "Perfect cut, perfect fit. Should have held for centuries." He lifted a fragment, showing Fidel hairline cracks. "The pressure was too much, too fast. Regulus rushed the foundation."

As they worked, Garus taught Fidel to read the story in broken stone. How mortar should flow. Why certain joints bore weight better than others. Which failures came from flawed materials versus flawed technique.

"Stone has its own nature," Garus explained, showing how some sections had held together even in collapse. "Push it beyond what it can bear, and it'll fail. But work with its strengths..."

Fidel studied the intact sections with growing understanding. "The bridge failed because Regulus made everyone fight their limitations instead of working with them."

"Exactly. A master builder knows his materials—stone and human both."

By afternoon, Fidel's hands were raw but his mind alive with new understanding. How foundations should be laid, why some structures endured while others crumbled.

"You've got good instincts for this work," Garus said. "If you want to learn more..."

"I do," Fidel replied. "Next time someone promises to build a bridge, I want to understand whether they know what they're talking about."

Garus smiled grimly. "If there is a next time, we'll be ready with real knowledge, not just hope."

That night, Fidel stood again at his signaling point, the wind tugging at his sleeves. His hands shook as he raised his lantern—not from cold, but from the tremor that had lived in his chest since watching the bridge collapse.

He drew a slow arc—

"Love."

A pause that felt like an eternity.

Then, across the river, the light returned—

"Love."

Something cracked open in his chest, and for the first time since the collapse, tears came. Not the bitter tears of rage or the hollow tears of despair, but something cleaner—the tears of relief.

She was still there. After everything—after Regulus's condemnation, after eleven months of impossible standards, after the catastrophic failure that had shattered his faith in effort itself—she was still there.

He added a triangle to the sequence—

"Laugh."

The response came without hesitation—

"Always."

And suddenly, he found himself smiling through his tears. Not because everything was all right—it wasn't. Not because the pain was gone—it still lived in his chest like a wound that would never fully heal. But because this simple exchange of light, this basic connection across the darkness, remained untouched by all of Regulus's requirements.

Whatever came next, this would endure. This light in the darkness. This love that needed no bridge, no standard, no proof of worthiness.

For now, that distant connection was all he had left.

# Chapter Five

## Sophia

### The Philosopher

Fidel stood alone at the shoreline, the first light of morning casting pale gold across the churning waters. The river still raged with unnatural fury—a violent torrent that had never calmed since the earthquake over a year ago. The sight of it always made his stomach clench with fear, but somehow he felt closer to Verita here, at the edge of the barrier that separated them.

Around him, tender spring buds were just beginning to emerge on the bare branches, and patches of new grass pushed through the last remnants of melted snow. He had come here to think after another restless night. The valley lay in a hush broken only by the wind and the constant roar of angry water.

His mind churned with the same questions that had tormented him since Regulus's bridge had collapsed months ago. How could they possibly build something strong enough to span this furious river? What were they missing? Why had they failed so catastrophically? There had to be something—some key, some principle, some knowledge—that could ensure their success in the future.

He tilted his head back and whispered into the open sky.

"Creator... if there's anything left. A sign. A clue. Something we've missed."

There was no reply—just the breeze moving through fractured stone and ash.

With nowhere else to go, he wandered toward the remains of the original bridge—the ancient span that had connected the shores for generations before the earthquake destroyed it. Just to pass the time. Just to breathe.

His hands brushed the weathered railing, the ancient stones cool beneath his fingers. As he neared the only remaining watch station, something odd caught his eye—a rusted edge beneath the bench, half-concealed by fallen timber.

He knelt to investigate. Wedged into a hidden compartment was a small metal container, aged but intact. His fingers fumbled with the latch, heart already racing. Inside, wrapped in timeworn cloth, was a scroll.

He stared at it, hardly daring to breathe. Then slowly, reverently, he unwrapped the cloth and unrolled the parchment. Symbols filled the page—rows of shapes, each one precise and purposeful. Patterns of light, movement, and meaning. Enemy. Shelter. Delay. Proceed.

A quiet laugh escaped him—astonished, breathless. Joy rose in his chest like light breaking over water. This is it. The full code. Not the fragments he and Verita had improvised. Not the handful of motions they'd clung to like lifelines. This was the language of the watchmen, hidden since the collapse, waiting to be found.

He immediately began studying it, learning its symbols, memorizing the movements, and practicing them with his lantern. Page after page of extra words, even phrases, practically sentences.

"Creator, if this was your answer... thank you."

The next evening, Fidel let forth a fury of signals to Verita. New ones they had not used. She caught on, recognizing the signals her uncle had taught her, and expressing gratefulness for their ability to communicate more deeply.

***

Several days later, as Fidel traced the familiar arc with his lantern in the early evening light, his movements now precise after months of practice, he became aware of someone watching him intently. A woman stood at the edge of the river, her silver-rimmed spectacles catching the lantern's glow.

She stepped forward as he finished his signaling. "Remarkable," she said, her voice carrying the measured cadence of scholarship. "A systematic communication across a far distance."

Fidel looked up, curious about this newcomer. She was middle-aged, with a cascade of dark curls and clothes that marked her as someone of learning—simple but well-made, with ink stains on her fingers and scrolls tucked under her arm.

"I am Sophia," she introduced herself with a slight bow. "A philosopher from the eastern provinces. I've come because of the stories carried by the exiles—those who fled after the earthquake, leaving behind shattered homes and broken lives. Stories of a broken bridge and of those still hoping to rebuild it."

Unlike Regulus, who had ruled with rigid certainty, Sophia brought scrolls—filled not with commands, but with questions. Her approach was not to instruct, but to inquire.

Where Regulus had arrived with cold authority, Sophia came with warm invitation. Her words flowed like honey, sweet with the promise of understanding. Where he had divided the community with his harsh standards, she promised to unite them with the allure of wisdom.

"If we can establish a more advanced signaling system," she explained, pointing to her diagrams, "we can expand your vocabulary, add complexity to your conversations. We can achieve deeper communication through logical inquiry."

A spark of hope kindled in Fidel's eyes. "You mean I could have actual conversations with her? Would that help us find a way to build a bridge?"

"Knowledge bridges all divides," Sophia said with a confident smile. "With proper communication systems and expanded vocabulary, we can achieve deeper connections across the river."

Fidel thought of the ancient scroll he had discovered that morning, now safely stored in his dwelling. "Let me show you something," he said, excusing himself to retrieve it.

He rushed to the small cottage he and his parents had been living in since the earthquake damaged their home—the roof partially collapsed and one wall cracked beyond repair. He returned with the ancient scroll, carefully unrolling the large parchment on the table before them.

Sophia's eyes widened. "Where did you find this?"

"Hidden in the original bridge," Fidel said. "Three days ago. Among the wreckage, in a watchman's station that was partially intact. The night watchmen had a way of signaling across—just simple things: 'all clear,' 'incoming cart,' 'changing post.' I remember seeing the lanterns flicker from my window as a boy."

Sophia's eyes lit with scholarly excitement. "This is remarkable! A signaling system developed over generations. And you say Verita knew these patterns too?"

He nodded. "Her uncle served on night watch for years. He taught her the basic signals during our courtship. She wrote them on a scroll so she has them, too. We added on to them, made them personal for us, and learned certain ways of saying them better with a lantern."

"Then we can build from this foundation," Sophia said. "Use the established code as a base, and layer in additional vocabulary, more complex concepts. We can give you a true language of light."

He nodded slowly, hope catching in his throat. Something in her words brought back a moment he'd treasured through all the dark nights since.

"I remember one night," he said quietly, eyes distant, "we lay under the sycamore tree and watched fireflies blink over the river. She said they looked like stars that had fallen just to be near us."

A soft smile touched his lips. "That night, we made a signal with our lanterns—a slow, gentle arc of light. It meant love. We used it every time we said goodbye."

His voice caught. "Now, after the collapse ... we've still been sending it."

Sophia listened, then carefully recreated the movement with her lantern—a smooth, deliberate sweep.

"Then we begin there," she said, "and slowly add in the vocabulary from this ancient code. Let's see if memory speaks louder than distance."

For the first time since the bridge collapsed, Fidel felt something more than hope—he felt the fragile stirrings of true reconnection.

***

As spring progressed into early summer—flowers blooming along the riverbank, birds returning to nest in the warming trees—the shoreline had transformed into an open-air academy. Canvas awnings shaded tables strewn with diagrams. Villagers came and went, watching, helping, hoping.

At the center stood the signal array—an intricate series of lanterns built on the ancient watchmen's code and carefully expanded into something more complex.

Each night, Fidel and Sophia sent carefully crafted messages across the river—signals rooted in shared history, the code of the night watchmen, layered with extra words that were learned from their light "vocabulary" as recorded in the Night Watchman's Code scroll.

The discovery of the complete Night Watchman's Code was revolutionising their communication. What had once been limited to simple words—love, miss you, always—had expanded into actual brief conversations. They could now ask questions, share further thoughts, and even describe daily events.

That evening, as light summer rain drummed softly on the academy's canvas roof, Fidel operated the primary lantern. Sophia stood nearby, recording every flicker and pause in her ledger. Villagers had gathered around them, drawn by word of the expanded communication system.

"Ask her about the day you proposed," Sophia urged.

Using the expanded vocabulary from the scroll, Fidel signaled a question about their engagement.

Moments later, a response came: a sequence that, according to the code, spelled out words she had spoken that day—"Yes for all time, in all seasons, through all trials."

Fidel's breath caught. The richness of detail, the specific memory shared between them.

"The expanded code is working," he whispered, his voice thick with emotion.

Sophia marked the response carefully in her ledger. "The complexity of that response shows how much deeper your communication can go with proper vocabulary." She adjusted her spectacles. "This is the power of knowledge—expanding what was already there."

For the first time since the collapse, Fidel felt not just connection, but genuine conversation flowing across the impossible divide.

"She's really there," he whispered. "We can actually talk."

An older woman wiped tears from her eyes. "It reminds me of how my husband and I would use our arms to signal to each other across the fields," she said. "Before he was taken in the collapse."

Others nodded, moved not just by the memory, but by the living conversation they were witnessing.

A younger man stepped forward, hesitant. "Could we ask about my sister?" he whispered. "She worked in the western infirmary."

Another voice—more urgent—called, "My nieces were visiting that week. Can you ask if they're safe?"

Soon, a quiet ripple passed through the gathered crowd—murmurs of names, of questions too long buried.

Fidel looked to Sophia. The expanded code made such inquiries possible now.

She hesitated, then gently closed her ledger. "One at a time," she said. "It will take time to craft signals, and more time to interpret replies. But we'll try."

A collective hush settled over the villagers. They were no longer just spectators of Fidel's hope. They had become participants in it.

"This is merely the beginning," Sophia continued, addressing the gathered villagers. "Through systematic inquiry and logical deduction, through the ancient knowledge we've rediscovered and constant learning, we are establishing true communication.

"Soon, we can use this expanded communication to coordinate bridge construction with the western shore—a bridge built not on rigid standards that no one can meet, but on perfect understanding of the principles of building anything that lasts: communication and connection."

As the villagers dispersed for the night, filled with a new sense of hope, Fidel remained at his usual signaling post on the shore. Using the expanded code, he and Verita had a brief conversation that would have been impossible just months before.

***

As the months passed and summer turned to early autumn, the advancing communication system had become the heart of village life. Families separated by the collapse exchanged detailed messages through the nightly signaling sessions. Short love notes crossed the void between spouses. Grandparents shared greetings with grandchildren they hadn't seen in over two years.

But Fidel found his patience wearing thin. "When do we start actually building?" he asked one crisp evening, as Sophia unfurled yet another diagram across the large central table. Nearly eight months had passed since her arrival, and while their communication system had grown, not a single stone had been laid for the new bridge.

Sophia looked up, her eyes bright with intellectual fervor. "We are building," she insisted. "We're constructing the most essential foundation—perfect understanding."

Around them, the academy bustled with activity. Villagers debated the philosophical nature of separation, the mathematical principles of structural integrity, and the symbolic meaning of bridges throughout human history. Knowledge flourished, but the river remained uncrossed.

"I need to reach her," Fidel insisted. "Not just communicate with her. I need to cross that river."

Sophia sighed, removing her spectacles to polish them with a silk cloth. "Regulus failed because he tried to build without understanding. I will not make the same mistake." She gestured toward an intricate model that dominated the central space of the academy, a bridge of such elegant design that it seemed almost too beautiful to be real.

"This is the Bridge of Reason," she explained, her voice taking on the cadence of a lecture. "Based on my analysis of river currents, available materials, and the principles of force distribution, it represents the perfect synthesis of theory and practicality."

Fidel studied the model. Unlike Regulus's rigid design, Sophia's bridge curved gracefully, its supports arranged in patterns that seemed to echo the natural flow of the river itself.

"When do we start?" he asked again.

"Tomorrow," Sophia promised, replacing her spectacles. "Now that the theoretical foundation is complete, we can begin the physical manifestation."

That night, using the vocabulary they had developed, Fidel sent urgent signals across the river.

"Bridge construction tomorrow. You safe?"

The response that came back, spelled out in the patterns of the ancient code, made his blood run cold:

"Danger here. Opposition to reunion. Someone working against bridge building. Be careful."

Fidel's breath caught. He steadied himself and sent another message:

"I'm coming. Hold on."

Then, as a final message, he added the ancient signal for eternal connection—a slow figure eight, meaning

"forever bound."

The reply came back with a pattern that meant

"faithful until death."

***

As autumn reached its peak, construction of the Bridge of Reason began with impressive ceremony and intellectual excitement. Unlike Regulus, who had rejected workers for the slightest imperfection, Sophia welcomed all contributions. Every villager was assigned a role based on their intellectual strengths; some calculated angles, others determined material requirements, still others translated the theoretical designs into practical instructions.

The bridge's foundation was laid with mathematical precision, each stone placed according to carefully calculated specifications. Progress seemed swift at first—the structure extending confidently from the eastern shore, its elegant curves a testament to the power of knowledge properly applied.

But as the weeks passed, something strange began to happen. What had started as a beautifully simple design began to grow more complex.

"I've been reconsidering the support structure," Sophia announced one morning, unfurling new diagrams that were significantly more elaborate than the original plans. "My latest calculations suggest we need additional reinforcement here, and here, to account for variables I hadn't initially considered."

The workers looked at the new designs with confusion. Where the original bridge had been gracefully simple, these new plans called for multiple layers of supports, elaborate viewing platforms for "educational purposes," and ornate decorative elements.

"But we've already built the foundation according to the first design," pointed out Garus, the lead stonemason. "Won't this require us to tear down what we've done?"

"Knowledge grows," Sophia replied, adjusting her spectacles. "We must be willing to improve our understanding, even if it means rebuilding. The pursuit of perfect comprehension requires such sacrifices."

And so they began adding elaborate features to the initial foundation, this time with the more complex design. But within days, Sophia had new insights, new improvements, and new theoretical advances that required further modifications.

As autumn deepened, the bridge had been redesigned four times. Each version was more intellectually sophisticated than the last, incorporating increasingly complex mathematical principles and philosophical concepts. What had begun as an elegant span had become a monument to human knowledge—decorated with carved equations, adorned with symbols representing various schools of thought, equipped with multiple observation decks for studying the river's flow.

\*\*\*

"We need to add a library section to the middle span," Sophia announced one crisp October morning, her eyes bright with new inspiration. "Imagine—travelers crossing the bridge could stop to study the principles that made their journey possible!"

"Think of the educational value!" Sophia exclaimed, spreading out yet another set of plans. "We could have scholars stationed there to explain the mathematical principles to visitors. It would be a bridge that teaches as well as transports!"

A man whose brother remained stranded on the western shore stepped forward, his voice tight with frustration. "Sophia, with respect, we've been working for months, and the bridge has barely reached a quarter of the way across. Every week you add something new."

"Because every week brings new understanding!" Sophia replied, seemingly oblivious to the growing tension in the crowd. "Would you have me ignore wisdom simply because it's inconvenient?"

The villagers exchanged glances. What had once felt like progress now felt like an endless spiral of intellectual elaboration. The bridge was becoming so complex, so laden with additional features, that actual forward movement had nearly stopped.

As the leaves began to fall, the village found itself divided into two camps.

Those who supported Sophia—mostly the educated merchants and craftsmen who enjoyed the philosophical discussions—gathered around her each evening to debate the latest theoretical advances. They spoke in increasingly complex terms about "structural semiotics" and "the philosophical implications of span-to-depth ratios."

But a growing number of villagers, led by Fidel and others desperate to reach their loved ones, began to meet separately.

"She's lost sight of the goal," Fidel said one evening to this second group. "The bridge isn't supposed to be a monument to human knowledge. It's supposed to get us across the river."

"My daughter's over there," a young woman said, tears in her eyes. "She's been waiting for over two years. I don't need a library in the middle of the river—I need a path to my child."

The division deepened daily. Sophia's followers, whom the others had begun calling "the Enlightened," spent their time in increasingly abstract discussions about the theoretical perfection of their designs. Meanwhile, "the Desperate," as they'd been labeled, watched helplessly as the bridge grew more elaborate but came no closer to spanning the divide.

It was during one of Sophia's lengthy lectures about "the epistemological foundations of structural engineering" that someone first noticed the stain.

Beneath her drafting table, where she had held court for months, a deep purple discoloration was spreading through the white stone of the work platform. It pulsed with an ugly rhythm, growing darker each time Sophia dismissed a practical concern in favor of theoretical purity.

"What is that?" asked a young apprentice, pointing at the spreading stain.

"Focus on the learning at hand," Sophia replied curtly, not even glancing down. "The principles of load distribution are far more important than cosmetic irregularities."

But the stain continued to spread, fed by her intellectual pride, her refusal to admit that her perfect understanding might be imperfect, her inability to see that knowledge without application was becoming its own form of tyranny.

***

By late autumn, work on the bridge had effectively stopped. Not because of any structural failure, but because every day brought new "insights" that required previous work to be reconsidered.

"I've discovered an error in our foundational assumptions," Sophia announced one gray November morning. "The entire western approach will need to be recalculated based on my new understanding of fluid dynamics."

The workers simply stared at her. They had rebuilt the same section twice already.

"That's it," a young worker said, throwing down his tools. "I'm done. My brother is over there, probably thinking I've abandoned him, while we build monuments to this woman's intellect."

One by one, others followed his lead. The construction site grew quiet as more villagers walked away from what had become an endless cycle of theoretical improvement and practical stagnation.

Sophia, left with only her most devoted followers, continued to work on increasingly elaborate plans. But with each passing day, fewer people came to listen to her lectures. The bridge sat partially built—perhaps a third of the way across—its elegant curves now burdened with so many decorative elements and educational features that it looked less like a means of transportation and more like a confused academic monument.

***

Winter arrived early that year, and with it came a bitter realization. The Bridge of Reason, for all its intellectual sophistication, was never going to reach the other side. Not because it couldn't be built, but because knowledge had become so full of itself that workers could no longer continue.

"We could start over," one of Sophia's remaining followers suggested hopefully. "Apply all we've learned to a simpler design."

But Sophia shook her head, her confidence finally shaken. "I don't understand what went wrong. The theory was sound. The knowledge was complete. Everything should have worked."

She gathered her scrolls and instruments, her face a mask of intellectual confusion. "Perhaps with more research, more data..." she murmured, but her voice lacked conviction.

Fidel approached her as she prepared to leave. "Sophia," he said quietly, "I want to thank you. The communication system you helped us develop, the expanded code—that was a real gift. We can actually talk across the river now, have actual conversations."

He paused, looking back at the unfinished bridge. "But knowledge alone... it wasn't enough to get us across. Knowledge became so proud of itself that it stopped building toward the goal."

Sophia nodded slowly, understanding dawning in her eyes. "I came to help you cross, but I became more interested in the perfection of the method than in reaching the destination." She adjusted her spectacles one final time. "I hope someone else can find a way where I could not."

Days after Sophia's departure, Fidel found himself in her abandoned academy. Scrolls and diagrams lay scattered across the tables. Most villagers avoided the site, but Fidel felt drawn to understand what she had attempted.

He picked up a bridge design covered in measurements and calculations. The symbols meant nothing at first, but remembering Garus's lessons about reading stone, he began to see patterns.

"Load distribution," he read, tracing lines from the bridge's center. "Stress concentration points." Hours passed as he taught himself to interpret the notation. Sophia's notes explained how weight traveled through bridges, why angles mattered, and how forces could be redirected.

"So that's why Regulus's design failed," he murmured, comparing diagrams with his memory of the collapse. The perfect angles had concentrated pressure where the foundation couldn't handle it.

By sunset, Fidel had filled pages with rough sketches, translating complex diagrams into simpler forms. Unlike Sophia, he wouldn't let knowledge become a prison. When the time came, he would use what he'd learned.

The villagers watched her leave on a cold December morning; her cart loaded with diagrams of bridges that existed only in the realm of perfect understanding. Behind her, the Bridge of Reason stood as a monument to knowledge that had become too proud to serve its purpose—elegant, sophisticated, and utterly useless.

***

That night, as the first winter winds began to blow, Fidel returned to the signaling spot alone. The elaborate signaling system Sophia had designed lay abandoned, but the essential knowledge remained—the ancient code that had always been there, waiting to be rediscovered.

He raised his simple lantern once more, using the expanded vocabulary the ancient scroll had provided.

"Construction stopped. Knowledge wasn't enough."

The response that came back was simple:

"Still believe. Still here. Love finds a way. Don't give up hope."

"I won't." "Learning stonemasonry and knowledge patterns." "Hope useful to reach you." "Heart is yours."

Until the stars burn out."

"Until the stars burn out," she replied. "And beyond."

As he watched the distant light, Fidel reflected on what they had gained and lost. Sophia's gift had been real—the expanded communication, the rediscovered code, the deeper connection across the void. But her pride had turned that gift into a burden, transforming a tool for reunion into a monument to human intellect.

The bridge remained unfinished, not because they lacked knowledge, but because knowledge without wisdom, understanding without humility, had become its own form of blindness.

Yet something in him stirred with quiet determination. Somewhere in the growing catalog of failures, there had to be a lesson that pointed toward truth. Not the truth of perfect understanding, but something simpler and more enduring.

As he prepared to leave his signaling post, Fidel sensed movement behind him. Turning, he saw a figure approaching through the gathering darkness. Unlike Regulus with his measuring tools or Sophia with her scrolls, this newcomer carried objects of a different nature—ornate ceremonial vessels, strings of sacred beads, and embroidered vestments that caught the moonlight.

The stranger's movements were deliberate, rhythmic—almost like a dance. Without speaking, the figure began arranging the ceremonial objects on the river's shore, lighting incense that sent fragrant smoke spiraling into the night air.

Only after completing these preparations did the stranger speak.

"I am Ritus," he announced. "I have journeyed here from the mountain monasteries to the north, where we have long preserved the sacred traditions. Word reached us through traveling merchants of your struggles—how the ancient bridge fell, how attempts to rebuild have failed. The elders sent me because they believe that what has been broken by earthly force can only be restored through heavenly ritual."

He gestured toward the ceremonial objects glowing in the moonlight. "The Bridge of Law failed because it demanded perfection without providing help. The Bridge of Reason failed because it offered understanding without power to transform. But the Bridge of Sacred Ritual will succeed where others have failed, because some traditions are beyond time, beyond corruption."

Fidel looked from the stranger to the distant light across the river, then back again. The ache in his heart to be with Verita drove him to listen and to watch this newcomer with hope.

In the darkness, Ritus began to chant, his voice rising and falling in ancient patterns that seemed to stir something deep in the collective memory of the village. Despite his skepticism, Fidel felt himself drawn to the hypnotic rhythm, the promise of connection through sacred tradition.

Across the river, using the expanded code they now shared, Verita's light flickered urgently—a warning that their enhanced communication made crystal clear:

"Be careful."

# CHAPTER SIX

# Ritus

## THE RITUALIST

The incense smoke coiled upward, fragrant tendrils weaving through the crisp winter air. Ritus stood at the river's edge, his embroidered vestments catching the pale light of the winter dawn. His hands moved in practiced patterns as he scattered dried flower petals into a small ceremonial bowl of still water he had brought, the petals floating in sacred arrangement while the churning river raged beyond.

"The ancients knew," he intoned, his voice resonant with practiced melody, "that to bridge any divide, we must first honor the spirits of the water, the blessing of the earth, and the sacred patterns that govern all construction."

Fidel watched with cautious interest, his breath visible in the cold air. After Sophia's failure just as winter had begun, he had retreated into solitude, spending hours at the riverbank despite the bitter cold. In his pocket, he carried a small carved wooden bird—Verita's engagement gift to him. His fingers traced its familiar shape, a ritual of remembrance that kept her close when everything else conspired to keep them separated.

Nearly two full years had passed since the original collapse. Two attempts, two failures. The village bore the scars not just of physical destruction, but of hope raised and shattered.

Something about the ritualist's approach reached parts of the village that neither Regulus's rigid standards nor Sophia's intellectual theories had touched. The ceremonies seemed to acknowledge their grief, to give form to their yearning, to create beauty amid devastation.

Word of the newcomer's arrival had spread quickly through the village. By evening, curious villagers had gathered in the square to hear what this latest arrival might offer.

"You've tried perfection through law," Ritus told the gathered villagers, their faces gaunt from the harsh winter that had followed Sophia's collapse. "You've tried perfection through understanding. Both failed because they addressed only part of what makes us human. We are heart, mind, and spirit," he said, touching his heart, then his head, then extending his hands upward. "Only by honoring all three can we hope to rebuild the bridge."

An old woman wept quietly as Ritus led them through a ceremony of remembrance, calling out the names of those lost in the bridge collapse. For each name, a small candle was lit and placed along the edge of the river, their flames flickering in the winter wind like souls refusing to be forgotten.

Near the edge of the crowd, Fidel noticed a familiar figure crouched behind the weaving stall. Timidia. Now fifteen, she had grown even more withdrawn during the years of failures, her youthful face marked by premature lines of sorrow. Her hands were clasped tightly in her lap, eyes fixed on the flickering candles with a longing that made Fidel's heart ache. She didn't join the procession, didn't light a candle, but mouthed the names silently as they were read—until one name made her flinch. Her lips stopped moving. Her eyes glistened.

Was it her brother? Cousin? Parents? Fidel didn't know. But her silence said everything.

When someone offered her a candle to light, she looked down, shook her head and backed away. Still silent. Still unseen.

When Ritus spoke Verita's name—not lost to death, but lost to separation—Fidel's breath caught in the cold air. Tears he hadn't allowed himself to shed for months suddenly flowed freely, freezing on his cheeks. For the first time since the collapse, someone had acknowledged his grief as real, as sacred.

"She waits," he whispered through his tears as his candle joined the others, his voice breaking. "She signals each night. But will I ever hold her again?" The ritual had cracked something open in his chest, a pain so long buried it felt like resurrection.

***

Throughout the remainder of that harsh winter, Ritus established increasingly elaborate ceremonies. Unlike previous bridge-builders, he insisted that spiritual preparation must come first.

"The bridge failed because the people were not ready," he explained during one of his evening gatherings as snow fell heavily outside. "Stone and mortar are useless if the souls who cross are not purified."

Fidel found himself drawn to these winter ceremonies despite his skepticism. Now twenty-four and aged by two years of disappointment, he appreciated the way Ritus honored the grief they all carried. But he also noticed how the ceremonies grew longer each week, more complex, requiring ever more precise observance.

That winter night, with ice forming along the riverbank, Fidel stood at his signaling post wrapped in a thick cloak. The cold made his hands stiff, but he maintained his nightly vigil. Thanks to the expanded Night Watchman's Code that Sophia had helped them discover, he and Verita could now exchange brief conversations rather than just simple signals.

He raised his lantern slowly, the familiar weight grounding him despite the bitter wind.

Using the expanded code, he signaled:

"Cold night. Miss warmth. Your touch."

Across the river, her light appeared, cutting through the winter darkness with a response that brought joy, and sadness, to Fidel:

"Same here. Fire burns. Heart empty."

The ability to share actual thoughts, even brief ones, made their separation both more bearable and more painful. He could hear her voice in the patterns now, not just feel her presence.

He continued:

"Builder arrived. Ceremonies help. Still doubt."

Her reply came thoughtfully:

"Different here. Builder focuses. Work practical. Trust together. Not methods."

Fidel smiled despite the cold. Even across the impossible distance, she saw through to what mattered. And it seemed both shores were attempting to build again, though with different approaches.

"Forever together, even when apart," he signaled, tracing a slow circle—their private signal representing the wedding band that would unite them.

"Forever together, even when apart," she replied with the same circular pattern.

\*\*\*

As winter slowly gave way to early spring, Ritus unveiled a model of a bridge unlike any they had seen before; not the rigid, perfect structure of Regulus nor the theoretically elegant design of Sophia. This bridge incorporated symbolic elements from countless traditions: small niches for prayer, carvings representing the elements, spaces for meditation, pillars inscribed with sacred texts.

"This," Ritus proclaimed as the first spring flowers began to bloom, "is the Bridge of Sacred Union. Not built merely of stone and wood, but of devotion, tradition, and faith."

The building site had been transformed by late spring. Prayer flags fluttered from poles surrounding the foundation. Stones were washed in sacred waters before being placed. Each morning began with ritual cleansing; each evening ended with songs of gratitude.

Unlike Regulus, who had rejected workers for their imperfections, Ritus welcomed everyone, assigning roles based on spiritual intuition rather than measurable skills. Unlike Sophia, who had divided tasks based on intellectual abilities, Ritus created teams that mixed abilities, ages, and backgrounds.

The bridge's foundation grew steadily through the warm months of summer, its decorative elements a stark contrast to previous attempts. Where Regulus's bridge had been coldly precise and Sophia's theoretically elegant, this structure had a living quality, almost as if it breathed with the workers who built it.

A young man whose arm had been crushed in Regulus's collapse stepped forward during one of the midsummer ceremonies, tears cascading down his face. "I felt whole again during the blessing," he said, flexing fingers that had been numb for months. "The pain is gone." Others murmured similar experiences; headaches lifted, old wounds that had festered were now clean. Even the cynical felt something stirring, a warmth they hadn't experienced since before the first collapse.

As the weeks of summer passed into early autumn, Fidel found himself unexpectedly drawn into the rhythms of the rituals. He still doubted much of the symbolism, but the sense of shared yearning gave the community something he couldn't deny—unity.

Each night, despite the growing demands of the ceremonial life, Fidel would run to the riverbank—waiting for her light, hoping for even one more moment of connection.

*** 

One evening in late summer, her lantern appeared almost immediately when he raised his.

Using the expanded vocabulary they now shared, Verita signaled: "Special day. Remember meadow. Ring hidden."

Fidel's hands stilled. *What day is she talking about?* he thought, searching his memory. Then it hit him—*Oh wait, it is the three year anniversary of when I proposed!*

The meadow. The afternoon sun. The ring hidden in my coat pocket. Today was the day. The day I asked her to be mine. She remembered.

He let out a shaky breath and responded with a small circle—

"Band." A wedding band, a symbol of their promise.

Moments later, her reply came: a triangle—

"Laugh."

He closed his eyes. *I miss your smile. I miss your laugh. I miss your touch. I miss the way you looked at me when the world fell quiet.*

He added one final signal:

"Always."

Their light dimmed, but the ache remained.

*** 

As autumn deepened and the rituals had grown increasingly complex and demanding, Fidel had noticed troubling patterns. What had begun as meaningful ceremonies now consumed more time than the actual building. When support beams cracked, it was because someone had spoken during sacred silence. When mortar crumbled, it was because the proper offerings hadn't been made. When workers fell ill from exhaustion, it was because they harbored secret doubts.

The bridge had been under construction for nearly a full year now, yet progress seemed to slow rather than accelerate. Every stone placement required a blessing. Every timber needed purification. Every joint demanded a ceremony.

That evening, as autumn leaves drifted past his lantern, Fidel was able to share his concerns more clearly than ever before.

"Bridge progress slow," he signaled.

"Rituals increase. Worry growing."

Her response came quickly:

"Building here too. Different approach. Problems."

More complex thoughts could now pass between them:

"Workers exhausted. Less building. More ceremony."

She replied:

"Here opposite. Too fast. No care. Rushed work."

The revelation that both shores were building, but with completely different problems, wasn't lost on him. Even their separate efforts seemed doomed to different kinds of failure.

"Love beyond words," he signaled.

"Words not enough," she agreed. "Hearts speak louder."

Later, as Fidel returned from his heartfelt time with Verita, he asked some workers who were rehearsing movements, "Do you understand why we do these particular rituals?"

They exchanged glances. "Because Ritus says we must," one finally answered. "The exact movements must be performed precisely, and miracles will happen."

Fidel recognized the echo of Regulus in those words—the same demand for perfection, only now cloaked in spiritual language.

The day of the Great Consecration arrived in late autumn, exactly one year after Ritus had first appeared. The leaves were turning gold and red, and there was a chill in the air that promised winter's return.

From the riverbank, the eastern bridge stretched far across the divide, and for the first time, they could clearly see the western bridge reaching toward them. The gap between the two structures had narrowed to perhaps thirty feet—close enough that voices could carry, though barely audible over the churning water.

Ritus had declared that this ceremony would imbue the structure with the final spiritual strength needed to reach the opposite bank. People had witnessed miracles throughout the year, and believed Ritus when he said that today the bridge would be complete.

The entire village gathered at dawn on the riverbank, dressed in ceremonial garments, their breath visible in the crisp autumn air. The bridge had been decorated with thousands of prayer flags, offering bowls, sacred symbols, and burning incense. Musicians played ancient instruments, their haunting melodies carrying across the water.

Ritus appeared, more elaborately attired than ever before. His vestments gleamed with golden embroidery, and his headdress rose in tiers of symbolic significance.

"Today," he proclaimed, "we complete what others have failed to achieve. Through perfect devotion, through sacred tradition, through the wisdom of the ancients, we will bridge the unbridgeable. It will be a miracle like no other. We will join our loved ones on the other side today."

Near him, a woman clutched a small portrait to her chest; her two children, lost on the western side nearly three years ago. "Today I hope to see them again," she whispered, her eyes bright with desperate faith. "The ritual will bring them home." An elderly man beside her nodded, his gnarled hands over his heart. "My grandson. He was only five when the bridge fell. He'll be eight now. This has to work. It has to."

*Please let this be the one. Let me hold her again. Let me feel her heartbeat against mine. I can't endure another failure...* Fidel thought desperately, his heart hammering against his ribs.

Hours passed. The sun climbed toward its zenith as the ceremony continued without pause on the riverbank. Sweat beaded on foreheads despite the autumn chill, voices grew hoarse from chanting, limbs ached from holding ritual postures.

Finally, as the ceremony reached its climax, Ritus led a procession onto the bridge itself. Fidel joined the village elders following him, each carrying a ceremonial object. They proceeded along the bridge to its farthest extension, where Ritus had established an elaborate altar decorated with autumn leaves and harvest offerings.

Now, standing at the bridge's end with the western shore visible just thirty feet away, Fidel could see Verita clearly for the first time in nearly three years. She stood at the edge of her bridge, her dark hair catching the sunlight, her eyes fixed on his. The builders on her side appeared to be ordinary craftsmen, their clothes practical rather than ceremonial.

"Verita!" he called out, cupping his hands around his mouth.

Across the gap, she waved, and though the words were barely audible over the river and the wind, he heard her voice calling back: "Fidel! I see you! I love you!"

"I'm here! I've waited!" she added, and this time her response was clear enough to understand.

Others began calling to their loved ones as well. The gap was narrow enough now that they could see faces, recognize gestures. After nearly three years of separation, families were tantalizingly close to reunion.

"From this sacred center," Ritus intoned, raising his staff high, "we call upon the powers that bind all things. With perfect devotion, with flawless ritual, with complete faith, we command this bridge to stand firm, to reach across, to reunite what was divided! Workers, begin laying the final stones!"

The blessed stones were brought forward, and workers began the delicate process of extending the bridge toward the western structure. Each stone was placed with ceremony, blessed with incense and sacred words.

Then Fidel felt it, a subtle vibration beneath his feet. The vibration grew stronger, accompanied by an ominous creaking sound.

The massive ceremonial structures that adorned the bridge—the elaborate altar, the heavy stone carvings, the ornate viewing platforms—had created a fatal imbalance. What Ritus had conceived as spiritual enhancement had become structural burden. The bridge was trying to support not just people standing, but a monument to ceremony itself.

A sharp crack echoed across the water as one of the ornate support pillars buckled under the weight of its own decorations.

Ritus stumbled mid-blessing, his eyes widening in horror. "No," he gasped. "The devotion was pure."

"Everyone off the bridge!" shouted one of the engineers, breaking sacred silence without hesitation.

The procession dissolved into chaos as people rushed toward safety. Fidel pulled Ritus forcefully, dragging him toward the shore as the bridge began to buckle and sway beneath them. They barely reached solid ground before the Bridge of Sacred Union gave way with a thunderous roar.

But this collapse was different from the others. Instead of the clean, complete devastation they had witnessed with Regulus's bridge, this structure came apart in sections. The weight of the elaborate ceremonial additions had created stress points throughout the span, and now those decorative elements were tearing the bridge apart from within.

As the villagers watched in horrified fascination, the bridge tore itself apart piece by piece. The central span with its elaborate altar crashed first, taking most of the ceremonial elements with it. Then the decorated middle sections collapsed in sequence, prayer flags and sacred symbols disappearing into the churning water.

When the destruction finally ended, the river had claimed nearly everything. But scattered across the water at irregular intervals, three massive stone monuments remained standing—isolated pillars that had once supported ceremonial platforms. They rose from the river like ancient tombstones, too heavy and deeply rooted to fall, but now serving no purpose except as reminders of what had been attempted.

The villagers stood in stunned silence, staring at the hollow monuments. Each pillar was carved with sacred symbols and inscribed with spiritual texts, beautiful and meaningless now that they stood alone in the rushing water. They were too far apart to serve any practical purpose, too isolated to reach, too permanent to ignore.

A woman's anguished cry cut through the silence: "My daughter's name was on those prayer flags; now they're at the bottom of the river with her memory!"

Another voice, bitter with recognition: "We built monuments to ceremony instead of a path to our loved ones. The ritual became more important than the reunion."

Fidel stared at the three lonely monuments standing in the water like grave markers. They were beautiful, ornate, perfectly crafted—and completely useless. "A year of our lives," he said quietly. "A year of ceremony and devotion, and all we have to show for it are three stone monuments to our own spiritual pride."

***

That night, as the first winter wind of the new season began to blow, Fidel returned to the riverbank alone. The three stone monuments stood silhouetted against the moonlight like grave markers, beautiful and utterly meaningless.

He raised his lantern with hands that trembled—not from cold, but from a grief that went deeper than the previous disappointments. Regulus's bridge had collapsed catastrophically, Sophia's bridge had been abandoned incomplete—but this one had turned their devotion into decoration, their faith into hollow monuments.

"Third failure," he signaled. "Heart breaking. Hope fading."

Her reply came slowly, heavy with shared sorrow:

"Saw collapse. Monuments remain. Empty beauty."

"Ceremony killed what ceremony claimed to serve," he continued, staring at the ornate pillars rising from the water.

She replied:

"Faith became performance. Lost the heart."

The communication felt different tonight—heavier, more bitter. They had watched ceremony devour meaning, watched ritual consume its own purpose.

"What now?" he asked, the question that had haunted him through three failures.

"Keep truth," she replied. "Not ceremony. Not performance. Truth."

Even in their shared disillusionment with sacred tradition, even with the hollow monuments mocking their faith, their simple exchange of light remained untainted.

"Always," he replied. "Until stars burn. And beyond."

"Until stars burn out. And beyond," she answered.

As he prepared to leave his signaling post, Fidel found himself staring at the three monuments standing in the water. Tomorrow, villagers would wake to see them—permanent reminders of how spiritual pride had consumed spiritual purpose, how their devotion had been transformed into decoration.

The monuments would stand there for years, he realized. Beautiful, carved with sacred texts, completely useless. They would become part of the landscape, a constant reminder that ceremony without heart becomes its own form of idolatry.

The next morning, Fidel found the village paralyzed by grief and confusion. Families wandered aimlessly among the wreckage, unsure how to begin cleaning up. The elaborate ceremonies that had defined their lives for a year had left no one prepared for practical action.

***

The next morning, Fidel found the village paralyzed by spiritual crisis and confusion. Families wandered aimlessly among the wreckage, their faith shattered after a year of elaborate ceremonies that had culminated in spectacular failure. Many questioned everything they had believed about sacred traditions.

"People don't know what to believe anymore," Elder Moriah said helplessly, gesturing at villagers arguing bitterly about whether any ceremony had meaning. "Ritus has fled in shame. Now they don't know how to pray, how to gather, how to find hope."

Fidel looked around until he spotted a familiar figure sitting alone on the steps of what had once been the ceremony platform. "Harmonia," he called gently.

She looked up, her ceremonial sash torn and muddy, her usually composed face etched with exhaustion. "Fidel, I...I don't know what to do. Ritus said my old ways were insufficient. That simple ceremonies couldn't honor the sacred properly."

"Your ceremonies were never simple," Fidel said, settling beside her. "They were honest. They served people instead of impressing them." He gestured toward the confused villagers. "Look around. We need you now."

Over the following days, Fidel found himself working alongside Harmonia to help
the community heal spiritually. She organized simple gatherings where people could
share their doubts and fears, while he coordinated practical support—ensuring families
had food, organizing work crews to clear dangerous debris, managing the logistics of
community meetings.

"Speak from your hearts," Harmonia encouraged during their first gathering, her
confidence returning as she fell back into her natural role. "No prescribed words, no
complex rituals. Just honest faith, however small."

Fidel discovered he had a gift for supporting her leadership while adding his own
strengths. When arguments broke out over what to believe, he listened to all sides
and found common ground. When despair overwhelmed people, Harmonia provided
spiritual comfort while he redirected energy toward rebuilding their sense of community.

"You two work well together," Elder Moriah observed as they organized a simple
harvest blessing—the first meaningful ceremony since Ritus's departure. "Like you
understand that faith and action should serve each other."

The community healing they fostered together was simple, honest, and restorative
in ways Ritus's elaborate productions had never achieved. Harmonia's spiritual wisdom
combined with Fidel's practical coordination helped people rediscover that true faith
didn't require perfect performance.

***

That night, across the unchanged distance, Fidel and Verita's simple lights still found
each other in the darkness—no ceremony required, no ritual demanded, just two hearts
refusing to let distance have the final word.

# CHAPTER SEVEN

# Altruia

## THE HELPER

The first winter winds carried the scent of defeat as they swept across the village square, scattering the last remnants of Ritus's elaborate ceremonial decorations.

Dawn found Altruia already at work among the debris. She had arrived the previous evening—not dramatically like the others, but quietly, carrying only a simple bag of supplies and a heart full of compassion. Word of the village's suffering had reached the northern settlements through traveling merchants: stories of repeated bridge failures, of families separated for years, of a community growing bitter with accumulated disappointment.

"I've come to help," she had said simply when the village elders questioned her. "Not to build or teach or lead ceremonies. Just to serve wherever there's need."

Now, while the village still slept, she moved quietly through its streets, leaving baskets of food at doorways and clearing wreckage from the previous day's bridge collapse. Her simple clothes bore stains of honest labor: mud on the hem, herbal remedies on the sleeves, river water dampening the shoulders from where she had helped tend to workers injured during the evacuation.

Fidel watched her from a distance, his mind weary with accumulated disappointment. Three times now, three times, he'd believed salvation and connection had come, only to watch hope crumble. Regulus's bridge had collapsed with death and injury. Sophia's bridge had been abandoned incomplete, dividing the community. Ritus's bridge had left them with beautiful but useless monuments in the river.

The failures had carved something hollow inside him, a cavity that ached with each breath. But this woman seemed different—she made no grand promises, claimed no special knowledge, offered no revolutionary methods. She simply served.

Before sleep last night, he had taken out the small collection of keepsakes from his time with Verita: the wooden bird she had carved, a pressed flower from the meadow where he had proposed, a scrap of fabric from her favorite dress. These tangible connections to her were both comfort and torment, reminding him of all he had lost and all he still fought to regain.

Now twenty-five years old, Fidel felt the weight of three years since the original collapse. Three failed attempts. Three times his hope had been raised only to be dashed against the rocks of human limitation.

Altruia straightened from tending a child's scraped knee and noticed his scrutiny. She offered a simple nod, neither demanding his trust nor shying from his doubt. When she spoke, her voice was quiet but clear.

"The bridge failed," she stated plainly. "But the people remain. They need help now."

"We've had enough grand promises," Fidel replied, approaching cautiously. "Regulus promised perfection through law, Sophia through understanding, Ritus through devotion. All failed. What do you promise?"

Altruia considered the question as she wrung river water from a cloth. "I promise nothing but to serve," she said finally. "I can only offer my hands to the work and my heart to those who suffer."

Before Fidel could respond, cries rose from a nearby home. A roof weakened by tremors from the bridge collapse had partially caved in. Without hesitation, Altruia ran toward the sound, Fidel following close behind. Together they helped extract a family from the rubble—no serious injuries, but fear and shock aplenty.

\*\*\*

As the winter days progressed, Fidel found himself working alongside Altruia, first clearing dangerous debris, then helping distribute food, then rebuilding damaged structures. Her approach to each task was the same: quiet, practical, thorough. No elaborate theories, no complex rituals, no rigid standards, just an attentive response to immediate need.

The expanded Night Watchmen's Code that Sophia had helped them expand proved invaluable for coordinating relief efforts. Altruia asked Fidel to help coordinate with the western shore about resources. She also adopted some of Ritus's ceremonies, not as magical guarantees but as meaningful expressions of shared values and mutual support during the harsh winter months.

By the winter solstice, when Fidel took up his lantern to signal across the river, he felt unsure what to send. No new bridge had been started. No grand plan unveiled. And yet... something had shifted. A quiet hope stirred—not because of strategies or designs, but because of Altruia's gentle, unwavering presence.

Using the expanded code, he sent:

"Love." "Remember." "Helper contributes much." "Focus on service to others."

Across the river, her light appeared with the expanded vocabulary they now shared:

"Love." "Remember." "Different here too." "Considering building bridge."

Fidel hesitated, then added their private signal:

"Laugh."

He had used this signal only a few times before—their private code for a memory from their courtship. They used to watch sunsets together, and Verita would always claim she saw the first star before he did, leading to playful arguments that ended in laughter and kisses. The "laugh" signal meant, "Do you remember our silly competitions? Do you remember how young and carefree we were?"

Her reply came:

"Band."

The signal for their wedding rings, but in this context it meant *Yes, I remember everything about us. I remember our promises.*

Then a long pause.

"Always." Fidel knew she meant, "And I will keep remembering, no matter how long this takes."

He smiled, even as a tear slipped free. *You still wear it. You still wait.*

But then her light returned again—sharp, stuttering. Not part of their expanded language.

Fidel's smile faded. His grip tightened. *That flicker... like before. When she tried to warn me. No shape. No code. Just presence.*

He didn't respond with a signal this time. He just stood there, lantern lowered, heart watching.

***

The winter months passed with Altruia's influence transforming the village in unexpected ways. Where Regulus had created divisions based on worthiness, she cultivated connections based on need and ability to help. Where Sophia had established hierarchies of intellect, Altruia recognized wisdom in unexpected places: the child who knew which wild plants soothed burns, the elder whose weather predictions proved surprisingly accurate.

As the first hints of spring appeared—snowdrops blooming white through patches of melting snow, the faint lengthening of days—Fidel began to wonder if they would attempt another bridge.

Each night throughout the winter, Fidel would signal to Verita using their expanded vocabulary. Brief conversations now replaced simple signals:

"Miss you deeply." "Winter feels long." "Helper builds trust between people."

But one evening in early spring, before he even raised his lantern, her light was already there—waiting.

She signaled quickly:

"Love." "Love." "Love." "Miss you." "Love." "Love." "Love."

Fidel's hand trembled.

*You're not just saying "Love,"* he thought. *You're pleading it. Shouting it in silence.*

He answered:

"Love." "Always." "Spring coming soon."

Then her lantern sent:

"Band." "Still wear yours." "Wait faithful for you."

Fidel touched the worn metal on his finger. *Yes. I still wear mine too.*

He closed his eyes, holding the ring to his chest.

*We're not just exchanging signals anymore. We're echoing ache.*

***

As spring blossomed, the village found itself divided between those who wanted to attempt another bridge and those who had lost all hope. Voices grew heated in the evening gatherings.

"We must try again," insisted one of the former stonemasons. "The western side is considering building again."

"And fail a fourth time?" replied an elder, his voice bitter with accumulated disappointment. "How many more disasters must we endure?"

Fidel found himself caught between these factions, but as he watched Altruia continue her quiet service—tending the sick, feeding the hungry, mending what was broken—an idea began to form.

"What if," he said one evening as they shared a simple meal, "we focused on healing our community first? Before we attempt another bridge, maybe we need to rebuild the connections between us."

Altruia looked up from her bowl, nodding thoughtfully. "The bridges between hearts must come before the bridge over water," she agreed. "Service to each other must become as natural as breathing."

\*\*\*

As spring blossomed into early summer, word came through the expanded Night Watchmen's Code that the western shore was considering another attempt. Verita's signals indicated:

"Planning new project." "Different leader here." "Practical design." "Community discussing."

This news spread through the village of Eastlight, rekindling hope.

By midsummer, the community pressure to attempt another bridge had grown overwhelming. The western shore's signals confirmed they were ready to begin construction, and many villagers felt they couldn't delay any longer.

A village meeting was called. Altruia attended but sat quietly in the back, offering no opinions about bridge construction—that wasn't her area of knowledge or calling.

"We need a new approach," declared one of the elders. "Not law, not philosophy, not ritual. Something practical."

"What about compassion?" suggested Fidel, thinking of how Altruia's service had begun healing the community's wounds. "A bridge built on love shown through action?"

The idea took hold. Unlike previous attempts with their single commanding leader, this would be a collective effort—practical, achievable, focused on service to those who would use it.

They chose a simple design: sturdy, straightforward, incorporating the wisdom learned from previous failures. But Altruia made one crucial suggestion.

"If we're building a bridge to serve people," she said quietly, "shouldn't we include places along the way where travelers can rest, where the injured can be treated, where those in need can find help? A bridge that serves as well as transports?"

An old man looked skeptical. "Won't that slow down the construction?"

Altruia smiled gently. "True compassion cannot hurry past suffering. We build not just to cross, but to care for all who would use this passage."

Work began that very day. But unlike previous attempts, construction alternated with the building of service stations. The first platform, barely a hundred feet from shore, became a supply depot and first aid station. The second, a few hundred feet further, included sleeping quarters for workers and a kitchen to feed them.

Each evening, Fidel signaled to Verita—his love, his longing, his steady presence, and now regular updates about their progress.

"Bridge growing." "Service stations helping." "Different approach this time."

She always responded with her own updates:

"Progress steady here." "Challenges continuing." "Hope growing slowly."

***

As summer deepened into autumn, the Bridge of Compassion had achieved something remarkable—it extended nearly two-thirds of the way across the river, farther than any previous attempt. But something unexpected had happened during its construction.

The service stations had grown into small communities of their own. What had begun as simple rest stops now housed permanent staff: cooks who prepared meals around the clock, healers who tended injuries and illnesses, teachers who educated the children of workers, craftsmen who maintained equipment and structures.

"We've done something wonderful here," Altruia said one crisp October morning, standing on the central platform that had become the bridge's administrative heart. Around them, dozens of people moved purposefully—tending gardens, preparing food, caring for the sick, teaching classes.

Fidel looked toward the western shore, still tantalizingly distant. "But we're not crossing," he said quietly. "We're...staying."

It was true. The bridge had become a destination rather than a passage. Workers who came to build remained to serve. Families who brought supplies stayed to help run the kitchens. Children who started as visitors became students in the bridge's schools.

"Look how much good we're doing," Altruia continued, gesturing to a group of elderly villagers receiving medical care they couldn't get on shore. "People who were suffering are now healed. Those who were hungry are fed. The lonely have found community."

"But Verita—" Fidel began.

"Is being served too," Altruia interrupted gently. "Through our nightly communications, you serve her heart with your faithfulness. Isn't that enough?"

Fidel felt something cold settle in his stomach. *No. No, it's not enough.*

That evening, using the expanded Night Watchmen's Code, he sent a different kind of message:

"Bridge extends far." "Service stations created." "Workers not returning shore."

Across the water, Verita's response came quickly:

"Bridge stopped here." "Leaders fighting constantly." "Cannot work together."

Then, more details:

"Arguments over methods." "Different groups formed." "Construction halted completely."

Fidel's heart sank. While they had been building service stations, the western shore had torn itself apart with infighting and disagreement. Their counterparts had failed not from outside opposition, but from their inability to cooperate with each other.

Fidel looked around at the bustling community that had grown on the bridge platforms. People who had come to build were now permanent residents, trapped in an endless cycle of service that kept them from their original goal.

"Bridge becomes village." "People staying permanently." "Original purpose forgotten."

Her reply was immediate: "Escape if possible." "Service trap dangerous." "Still love you."

***

By the onset of winter, Fidel realized the terrible truth. The Bridge of Compassion had succeeded too well. It had become a self-sustaining community that consumed its own builders. Every day brought new people in need of service, new problems requiring attention, new reasons why the workers couldn't leave their posts to continue building.

"We can't abandon the sick," said a young woman who had come to build but now ran the medical station. "Who will care for them if we leave?"

"The children need their teachers," added another worker who supervised the bridge's school. "We can't just walk away from our responsibilities."

"Someone has to prepare the meals," insisted a third voice, from someone stirring a massive pot of soup. "These people depend on us."

Altruia nodded approvingly at each excuse. "You see? True service never ends. There will always be more to do, more people to help. This is our calling now."

Fidel stood at the bridge's farthest extension, staring across the remaining gap toward the western shore. So close. They were so tantalizingly close that on clear days he could see individual figures moving about. But the bridge would never be completed because all the workers were now permanently committed to maintaining the service community that had grown like a parasite on their original dream.

"I have to leave," Fidel announced that evening at the community meeting. "I came here to cross the river, not to build a floating village."

Gasps echoed around the platform. Altruia's face fell with disappointment.

"But the children in the school look up to you," she said. "The workers in the kitchen depend on your help distributing supplies. How can you abandon your service to this community?"

"Because service that turns inward stops growing outward," Fidel replied, feeling the truth of it in his bones. "We've built something beautiful here, but we've stopped reaching toward the other side. The bridge was meant to grow toward reunion, not become a destination in itself."

Others began to murmur agreement. The initial purpose had been lost in the endless demands of the service community.

"I'm going with him," declared Gareth, one of the lead stonemasons. "I came here to build a path to my daughter on the other side, not to become a permanent caretaker of this floating town."

One by one, more workers stepped forward. They had all come to cross the river, not to become permanent residents of a bridge community.

Altruia watched with growing dismay as her carefully built service community began to dissolve. "You're abandoning people who need you," she pleaded. "How can you be so selfish?"

"Sometimes," Fidel said gently, "the most loving thing is to help people reach beyond themselves toward their true destination. We've created a wonderful community here, but we've stopped growing toward the other shore. Service is beautiful, but when it becomes the end goal rather than part of the journey, we stop moving forward."

***

That night, as autumn winds howled around the bridge platforms, Fidel sent his final message from the Bridge of Compassion:

"Leaving bridge tomorrow." "Service trap recognized." "Workers returning home."

Verita's response came quickly:

"Brave choice made." "Service without goal." "Becomes prison bars."

Fidel smiled sadly. Even across the distance, she understood.

"Love beyond service." "Goal is reunion." "Coming home now."

Her final reply brought tears to his eyes:

"Waiting here always." "Love finds way." "Home in heart."

***

The next morning, Fidel joined the exodus from the Bridge of Compassion. Nearly half the workers left with him, finally choosing their original goal over the comfortable but purposeless service community that had grown around them.

As they walked back toward shore, Fidel looked over his shoulder at the bridge platforms still bustling with activity. Altruia remained, along with those who had become too deeply invested in the service roles to leave. The floating community would continue—serving many people well, providing genuine help to those in need, functioning as a valuable extension of Eastlight itself.

It wasn't a failure in the traditional sense. The Bridge of Compassion had become exactly what Altruia had envisioned: a place where the sick were healed, the hungry fed, the lonely given community. It would remain active, continuing its good work for years to come.

But it was not a bridge to the other side.

"Another failure," muttered one of the departing workers.

"No," Fidel said quietly, touching the wooden bird in his pocket. "Another lesson. Service is beautiful, but when service becomes the end goal rather than part of the journey toward reunion, we stop growing. We learned that love sometimes means choosing to reach beyond good things to pursue the best thing—connection with those we're meant to reach."

The bridge remained behind them—two-thirds complete, serving many people well, but ultimately a monument to how even the most compassionate intentions could lose sight of their true purpose.

That evening, back on solid ground, Fidel raised his lantern toward the western shore with hands that trembled not from defeat, but from hard-won wisdom.

"Still coming to you." "Different path needed." "Love finds way."

Across the water, her light appeared with a message that made his heart sing:

"Always believing that." "Always waiting here." "Love never gives up."

# CHAPTER EIGHT

## Optimus

### THE SELF-BELIEVER

The first autumn leaves were beginning to turn when a voice rang out across the village square, cutting through the September morning air with magnetic confidence.

"The only true limitation is the one you place upon yourself," Optimus declared, his voice carrying effortlessly to every corner of the spontaneously gathering crowd. "Look at me! I crossed the river without any bridge at all, through the power of my own belief."

Unlike previous would-be saviors, Optimus radiated an almost supernatural confidence. He carried nothing—no tools like Regulus, no scrolls like Sophia, no ceremonial objects like Ritus, no servant's basin like Altruia—just himself, seemingly complete and self-sufficient. His clothes were immaculate despite apparent travel, his posture perfect, his smile unwavering.

Fidel watched warily from the back, extremely cautious after four failed attempts over four years. Now twenty-six years old, having lived through repeated disappointments, he had learned to recognize the telltale signs of false hope. The villagers, however, leaned toward Optimus like flowers tracking the sun, desperate after watching Altruia's bridge become a permanent floating community that trapped people in endless service instead of enabling them to reach the other shore.

"How did you cross without a bridge?" someone called out, voice trembling with desperate hope.

"I refused to accept the river as my barrier," Optimus explained, his smile widening to encompass the entire crowd. "I visualized myself on the other side with absolute certainty, and the universe had no choice but to manifest it."

The crowd stirred with excitement, some green with envy. After four failures, after nearly four years of separation, someone claimed to have found the secret that had eluded all others.

"But why build a bridge at all if you can simply cross through belief?" called out a skeptical voice from the crowd.

Optimus's smile never wavered. "An excellent question! You see, manifestation without form is the highest level of spiritual development. Most of you are not yet ready to abandon physical supports entirely. The bridge will serve as your training ground—a way to strengthen your belief muscles until you can transcend material limitations altogether. Only when you reach the higher levels of faith can you leave such physical crutches behind."

One crisp October afternoon, when doubts about Optimus's methods and his supposed bridge-crossing were beginning to surface among the more skeptical villagers, Fidel encountered him alone by the remains of the original broken bridge. The usually immaculate self-believer appeared momentarily unguarded, staring into the churning water with an expression that didn't match his uplifting speeches.

"Do you ever doubt?" Fidel asked directly, his breath visible in the cooling air.

Optimus turned, surprise flickering across his face before his practiced smile reasserted itself. "Doubt is poison," he replied automatically. Then, looking down at the water, added more quietly, "At least, that's what I tell myself."

"What do you mean?"

Optimus hesitated, then sat on a nearby stone worn smooth by years of weather. "I wasn't always—" he gestured to his perfect appearance "—*this*. I was small, overlooked. Afraid." His voice had lost its performative confidence. "When you've been invisible your whole life, you either disappear completely or...reinvent yourself entirely."

"So all this—the confidence, the certainty...," Fidel asked.

"Began as an act," Optimus admitted, "until I could no longer distinguish between the performance and myself." He looked at Fidel with unexpected earnestness. "But it worked. People listened. They believed. And when they believed in me, I could finally believe in myself."

"But did crossing the river really happen as you claimed?" Fidel pressed.

The mask slipped back into place. "Reality is what we make it," Optimus declared, standing to straighten his clothes. "That's all that matters."

As he walked away, Fidel realized he'd glimpsed something genuine beneath Optimus's fabricated persona—not just a symbol of deceptive self-belief, but a wounded soul who had found the only power he could in a world that had once rendered him powerless.

*** 

That evening, Optimus held his first scheduled public gathering in the village square. The crowd that assembled showed clear signs of the community's growing despair after four years of failed attempts. The tavern now stayed open through dawn, filled with those drowning memories in drink. Once-unified families avoided each other, bitter over supporting different failed approaches. Some youth had turned to reckless pleasures of impurity, as if tomorrow might never arrive.

"After so many failures, how could you not doubt?" Optimus asked the assembled villagers, his voice carrying across the square. "But what if both the problem and the real solution were never explained to you? What if the power has always existed within you? As we begin to build a bridge that will last, visualize yourself full of power and light."

Even Fidel, watching from the edge of the gathering, felt pulled by these words—the seductive promise that he held the key to reaching Verita through belief alone, simply by accessing power the Creator had placed within.

As the crowd eventually dispersed at dusk, Fidel noticed something troubling. Optimus's shadow stretched toward the departing villagers like grasping fingers, despite the angle of the setting sun. More disturbing was how no one else seemed to notice.

That night, Verita's light appeared almost instantly—as if she had been waiting with unusual urgency.

Fidel raised his lantern and traced the expanded vocabulary they now shared:

"New arrival. Claims crossing. No bridge method."

A pause.

Then came her reply:

"Deception if shadow moves wrong."

He felt it in his chest—her urgency. Her warning.

He signaled:

"How resist influence?"

There was a long pause. Then two signals came—clear, steady: "Together always. Forest fire memory."

Fidel stared at the flickering light, breath catching.

The forest fire, he thought. She remembers.

He could almost smell the smoke again—thick and suffocating, the air so hot it seared their lungs. They had run in panic at first, separating in the chaos, nearly lost. But when they'd found each other—hands clasped, hearts steady—they had made a plan. Moved together. Covered each other. Found the stream. Found life.

We only made it out because we faced it together.

He answered with their most intimate signals:

"Love deeper than fear. Heart holds yours. Remember strength together."

Her reply came after a quiet pause:

"Always faithful. Always yours. Until stars burn."

Fidel lowered his lantern, eyes still on the shore beyond the dark river. He couldn't feel her hand, but he could feel her strength across the impossible distance.

And sometimes, that was enough.

***

As October turned to November and the first frosts painted the village silver, Optimus transformed the village center into a "Circle of Manifestation." Villagers sat in concentric rings, eyes closed, repeating affirmations: "I am powerful beyond measure," "The river yields to my will," and "My thoughts create my reality."

The community quickly divided. Believers spoke with pitying condescension about the "fear-bound" who couldn't join them. Those who questioned were labeled as "negative influences" and gradually ostracized from village life.

"He's changing them," Fidel remarked to Unitas one grey November evening, as they watched another manifestation circle form in the square. The elder had been Fidel's anchor since the original collapse—bringing him food when grief stole his appetite, sitting in wordless companionship through the longest nights, listening to him speak endlessly of Verita.

"I've been searching our oldest texts," Unitas replied, his gnarled hands sorting herbs by lamplight. "They warn of entities that feed on human desperation, beings that appear as light but cast shadows of darkness."

Despite his suspicions cast by the shadows, Fidel couldn't deny Optimus's appeal. The promise that he possessed everything needed to reach Verita was intoxicating.

During one visualization session in early December, as snow began to fall outside, Verita seemed so present that Fidel could almost smell the lavender in her hair.

The next evening, against his better judgment, he found himself drawn back to the Circle of Manifestation. He told himself he was only observing, gathering evidence of Optimus's deception. But as the rhythmic chanting began, as dozens of voices rose in unison declaring their power over reality, something loosened inside him.

"Close your eyes," Optimus instructed, his silky voice seeming to speak directly into Fidel's mind. "See her face. Feel her presence. She's calling to you across the void."

Fidel's eyes fluttered shut before he could stop himself. And there she was—not a memory, not a hope, but Verita herself, standing before him with perfect clarity. Her chestnut hair caught phantom sunlight, her eyes crinkled with the smile he'd dreamed of for over four years. She reached for him, her fingers warm against his cheek.

"I've been waiting," she whispered, her voice so real it made his chest ache. "Why do you signal across darkness when I'm right here? Why do you cling to suffering when joy is this simple?"

Fidel gasped as his eyes snapped open. Around him, other villagers swayed in peaceful rapture, their faces radiant with whatever visions danced behind their closed lids. For a moment—a terrible, wonderful moment—the illusion had felt more real than the cold stone beneath his feet, truer than the ache of separation he'd carried for years.

What if I'm wrong about everything? The thought struck him in the gut. What if Verita's nightly signals were just my imagination? What if I'd been clinging to delusion while she waited here, reachable through belief alone?

A drunken man stumbled toward the circle. "More lies!" Garus shouted—once the village's finest mason, now hollow-eyed with grief. "My family died in these attempts! How many more must die before we accept that we're meant to remain divided?"

When challenged to prove his crossing ability, Optimus's face flickered with something—anger? fear?—before he explained smoothly, "Manifestation requires alignment of belief. Your doubt creates resistance."

Later, Unitas revealed his discovery to Fidel. "The oldest texts mention the Deceptor, who feeds on human despair. Its tell is a shadow that moves independently, reaching for those it seeks to influence."

The description matched exactly what Fidel had observed, and what Verita had warned about.

***

As winter deepened and construction began in earnest, the work proceeded with surprising speed but alarming recklessness. Workers visualized their sections before building, applying minimal planning but boundless enthusiasm. The bridge grew rapidly through December and January, each worker convinced their positive thinking was strengthening the materials themselves.

"Your doubt creates the very flaws you perceive," followers told Fidel when he raised concerns about structural integrity during a particularly cold February morning.

The community fractured further as the months passed. Some abandoned essential duties for manifestation circles, others pushed themselves to physical collapse, believing exhaustion was merely a limiting belief. Most troubling were those who turned to destructive habits—excessive drinking, reckless gambling, and violent outbursts—unable to embrace Optimus's teaching yet seeing no alternatives after four previous failures. Some even took their own lives, leaving behind notes speaking of unbearable despair.

As the workers labored through the harsh winter months, a strange phenomenon began to appear. Where builders competed most fiercely—jealous of others who seemed to manifest better results or gain more favor with Optimus—a sickly green stain began to seep through the mortar like spilled bile. When questioned about it, Optimus dismissed it as "manifestation energy" made visible.

The green stains deepened wherever workers envied each other's apparent success. One section, built by a team consumed with jealousy over another group's faster progress, turned an unnatural emerald that hurt to look upon for long.

Spring arrived early that year, and with it came renewed fervor for the project. By April, the bridge extended farther than any previous attempt—nearly three-quarters of the way across the river.

Each evening, Fidel maintained his faithful vigil, signaling to Verita with their ever-expanding vocabulary.

On a warm April night, he sent:

"Bridge extends far now. Danger grows stronger. Deceptor feeds on hope turned bitter."

Her response came quickly, their communication now rich with nuance:

"Same deception here. Feeds on weakness after defeat. Grows stronger with each failure counting."

Fidel's breath caught. He stared into the darkness, lantern lowered. *She's watching the same pattern from her side,* he realized.

Perhaps she had seen what he was beginning to sense—people pulling back after repeated defeats, confidence unraveling, builders giving up hope. And in that vacuum of despair, something dark expanding its influence—not through supernatural power, but through the simple fact that people stopped believing anything else could work.

He signaled: "Why no building from your side?"

After a pause, her reply came:

"Leaders say wait. Let eastern bridge prove first. Too many false hopes broken. People afraid to believe again."

So her side was being cautious, Fidel realized. Learning from repeated failures.

He signaled:

"Grand ceremony planned soon. Feels dangerous."

After a long pause, her reply came:

"Spectacle equals risk always. Stay low profile. Protect heart space."

*Stay low? Protect heart space?*

It wasn't strategy—it was the wisdom of someone who had learned caution through painful experience. Don't draw attention. Don't get swept up in the moment. Guard the sacred places within.

Maybe she had seen ceremonies like this before—full of spectacle and promises, followed by manipulation and collapse. Maybe she had felt the pull herself. Whatever she had witnessed, it was enough to make her wary.

He nodded, eyes still fixed on the silent river. *She's not warning me like a leader. She's protecting me like someone who loves me.*

He added their most intimate signal:

"Love beyond doubt. Always faithful heart."

Her light answered after a gentle pause:

"Wedding band promise. Still wear yours. Still believing reunion possible."

He lowered his lantern with both hands, filled not with fear but with quiet strength.

\*\*\*

Through the summer months, the bridge construction accelerated at an almost supernatural pace. By late July, workers had completed the foundation and were rapidly extending the span across the river. The speed was intoxicating—after years of watching bridges grow slowly only to fail, this one seemed to leap forward with each passing day.

But with the rapid pace came corners cut, materials approved without proper inspection, joints that looked solid but lacked adequate support. When Fidel raised these concerns, Optimus would lead the entire workforce in visualization exercises.

"See the bridge as perfect," he would instruct, his eyes closed in apparent rapture. "Feel its strength flowing through every timber, every stone. Your positive thoughts are creating reality itself."

The workers would nod eagerly, convinced that their mental energy was somehow compensating for the shortcuts they were taking. When support beams showed early signs of stress, they were told these were merely "manifestations of doubt." When joints appeared loose, workers were instructed to "visualize them as tighter than steel."

As autumn arrived, the bridge had reached an unprecedented three-quarters of the way across the river—farther than any previous attempt. The completion ceremony was scheduled for the one-year anniversary of Optimus's arrival, and excitement in the village reached fever pitch.

But Fidel had begun to notice troubling signs. The bridge swayed more than it should in moderate winds. Several support timbers showed hairline cracks that were growing wider each week. Most concerning, some of the foundation stones had shifted slightly, creating gaps that should have been immediately addressed.

When he brought these observations to Optimus, the response was swift and dismissive.

"Your negative focus is creating the very problems you perceive," Optimus declared in front of the assembled workers. "Stop projecting failure onto our magnificent creation."

The workers cheered their agreement, but Fidel noticed several experienced builders exchanging worried glances. They saw what he saw but were afraid to speak up, having watched others be ostracized for expressing doubt.

Through the autumn months, the deterioration became impossible to ignore—at least for those willing to see it. The bridge's swaying had become pronounced enough that workers felt queasy crossing certain sections. The cracks in support beams had widened into visible gaps. Several foundation stones had settled noticeably, creating a dangerous instability that grew worse with each passing week.

But Optimus's response was always the same: "These are illusions created by fear-based thinking. We must maintain perfect faith in our creation."

When a section of railing broke away and fell into the river during a windstorm in November, Optimus declared it a "symbolic release of old limitations." When workers reported feeling the bridge move beneath their feet, they were told this was "energy responding to our elevated consciousness."

The cognitive dissonance became painful to watch. Workers would return from the bridge with obvious concern, only to participate in visualization circles where they convinced themselves everything was perfect. The gap between reality and belief grew wider each day.

By December, some of the more experienced builders began quietly refusing to work on certain sections of the bridge. A few brave souls approached village elders with their concerns, but Optimus's influence had grown so strong that dissent was quickly silenced.

"If the bridge fails," he proclaimed during one of his evening gatherings, "it will be because doubt poisoned the minds of the workers. We must maintain absolute faith in our vision."

This statement sent chills through those who remembered similar words from previous failed attempts. The bridge was no longer being built; it was becoming a test of faith that no one dared to fail.

As winter deepened, the signs of structural failure became undeniable. An entire section of decking sagged visibly. Support cables showed fraying that could be seen from the shore. The bridge's movement in wind had become so pronounced that birds avoided flying near it.

But Optimus forbade any inspections or repairs, declaring that such actions would "demonstrate lack of faith in our manifestation." Workers were instructed to simply visualize the bridge as perfect while avoiding looking too closely at any potential problems.

On a bitter February morning, exactly eighteen months after construction had begun, a weathered village elder whose trade involved assessing structural soundness—his calloused hands bearing the marks of decades spent testing stone and timber—made an announcement that sent shockwaves through the community.

"I'm officially condemning this bridge as unsafe for human passage," he declared, his weathered face grave with responsibility. "The foundation has shifted beyond acceptable limits. Multiple support structures show critical stress fractures. The deck sags dangerously in several locations. Anyone who attempts to cross risks serious injury or death."

The crowd fell silent. After eighteen months of relentless positive thinking, after visualizing perfection and manifesting success, their bridge—which had come closer to completion than any previous attempt—was being declared a failure before it even opened.

Optimus's response was swift and furious. "This man is a prophet of doom!" he declared, his perfect composure cracking for the first time. "He cannot see past his own limiting beliefs to recognize our achievement!"

But practical reality had spoken louder than positive thinking. Even Optimus's most devoted followers could see the bridge swaying in the wind, could notice the visible cracks and gaps, could feel the instability beneath their feet.

The Bridge of Self-Belief stood as a monument to ignored warning signs—nearly complete but utterly unusable, a dangerous structure that would remain as a permanent reminder of what happened when positive thinking replaced practical wisdom.

That night, as late winter winds howled around the condemned bridge, Fidel's hands trembled as he raised his lantern.

"Bridge condemned unsafe. Closest to completion ever. Failed through willful blindness."

A pause.

Then Verita's light returned:

"Saw deterioration from here. Warning signs ignored for months. Positive thinking cannot repair structural flaws."

He nodded, throat tight. She had watched it happen. Seen the slow decay that everyone on his side had been forbidden to acknowledge.

"Eighteen months of work. Useless monument now."

Her reply came thoughtfully:

"Sometimes failure gradual. More dangerous than sudden collapse. Harder to recognize."

Fidel stared at the darkened bridge stretching uselessly across the water—so close to the other side, yet permanently cut off by its own creator's refusal to face reality.

"How distinguish hope from delusion?" he asked.

A long silence stretched across the water.

Then her reply came with careful deliberation: "Hope sees problems and works to solve them. Delusion refuses to see problems at all."

With trembling hands, he signaled:

"Still real between us? Our connection across darkness?"

Her response came without hesitation:

"Real as sunrise. Real as heartbeat. Real as love that chooses truth over comfort."

As Fidel prepared to leave his signaling post, he reflected on the bitter lesson of Optimus's bridge. Unlike the dramatic collapses of previous attempts, this failure was more insidious—a slow rot disguised as success, problems ignored until they became irreparable, positive thinking used as a substitute for honest assessment.

The bridge would stand there for years as a warning: the closest any attempt had come to success, yet completely useless because its creator had chosen comfortable illusion over difficult truth.

Five attempts had failed. Five years had passed. And still, across the dark water, a faithful light waited for his signal each night—the one constant in a world of broken promises and shattered dreams.

But now Fidel carried something new: the hard-won wisdom that hope without honesty was just another form of despair, and that true love required the courage to see clearly, even when the truth was painful to bear.

# CHAPTER NINE

# Metamorphia

## THE CHANGER

The village square stood empty following Optimus's condemned bridge, the promised celebration replaced by the weight of yet another crushing disappointment. Fidel sat alone by the river's edge, his fingers tracing the worn edges of the wooden bird Verita had carved. Each night, his signals grew more desperate; each night her answering light sustained him through the darkness that followed.

At twenty-seven, Fidel bore the weight of half a decade's crushing disappointments etched into every line of his face. He had learned to recognize the signs of his own desperation. The night before, as spring's first warmth had settled over the valley, he had traced a slow arc—

"Love."

Then added a signal they hadn't used in awhile—"Heart."

Across the river, her light returned:

"Heart." "Always."

He closed his eyes. *You feel it too,* he thought. *Even from here.*

\*\*\*

"I HAVE SHED THE CHRYSALIS OF FALSE IDENTITY!" a powerful voice rang across the village square, drawing curious onlookers from every direction. "THE WOMAN YOU KNEW AS WEAK AND INVISIBLE NO LONGER EXISTS!"

A gathering formed near the village center, murmurs of excitement and confusion rippling through the crowd. At its heart stood a figure that caused Fidel to pause in bewilderment. The voice was commanding, authoritative, completely unfamiliar—yet something about the stance seemed familiar, though he couldn't place it until she turned, revealing her face.

A collective gasp went through the crowd. "Isn't that Timidia?" someone whispered nearby, their voice filled with disbelief. "The weaver's daughter who could barely speak above a whisper?"

Indeed, it was Timidia—once known for her hunched shoulders and downcast eyes, and for the way she seemed to apologize for her very existence. But the woman who stood before them now bore little resemblance to that former self. She stood tall, her gaze direct and unwavering, her voice commanding attention without effort.

Even her appearance had changed. Her once-drab clothing had been replaced with vibrant garments that flowed around her powerful frame. Her hair was styled dramatically, framing features now accentuated with bold colors that demanded to be seen.

"I am Metamorphia," she announced, her voice carrying across the square with an authority that silenced all whispers. "The woman you knew as Timidia no longer exists. I have completely transformed my very essence. I will never be invisible again—not like when my brother died and no one noticed me."

Fidel approached cautiously, remembering Verita's warnings about trusting too easily. Yet this was not a stranger arriving with grand promises—this was someone from their own community, transformed beyond recognition.

"How?" asked an elder, voicing the question on everyone's mind. "How did you become... *this*?"

Metamorphia's smile carried the confidence of someone who had discovered a profound truth. "By embracing who I truly am beneath the labels society forced upon me. I was never meant to be Timidia; small, afraid, insignificant. I simply needed the courage to become who I always knew myself to be." She gestured dramatically toward the river. "And if I can transform so completely, imagine what we could accomplish together!

My brother died when the first bridge collapsed, and my sister—my only family left—was visiting the western side that week. She's been trapped there ever since, the only person who truly knew me, who saw strength in me when no one else did. She always knew who she was, never doubted herself like I did. I need to reach her—we need to grieve our brother together, to be the family we have left. But a bridge built by people living as their authentic selves, as who we truly are meant to be—that is a bridge that cannot fail! We will cross not as broken, fearful people, but as our true, powerful selves."

Her words fell on a divided community. After five failed attempts to rebuild the bridge over many long years, some villagers craved any hope, any new approach. The accumulated weight of Regulus's perfectionism, Sophia's intellectualism, Ritus's empty ceremonies, Altruia's service that trapped people in endless helping instead of crossing, and Optimus's self-delusion had left many hungry for something—anything—that might finally work.

But others had grown hostile to any new promises. "How many more lies must we endure?" called out an elder, his voice bitter with accumulated disappointment. "How many more false promises will we follow to disaster?"

"No more bridges!" agreed a woman whose husband had been injured in Regulus's collapse. "We've heard these promises before. They all end the same way—in failure and heartbreak."

A rumble of agreement passed through part of the crowd, while others leaned toward Metamorphia with desperate hunger for hope.

"Each of us holds the power to transform," Metamorphia continued, her gaze sweeping across the gathered faces. "We are not who others tell us we are. We are not even who we appear to be. We are who we feel ourselves to be—whoever or whatever that might be."

\*\*\*

That night, Fidel raised his lantern into the dark.

"Timid young girl." "Totally changed." "Says can build bridge as true self."

Across the river, her light came slowly—more cautious than before:

"Not all change builds." "Watch closely."

He nodded, lantern pressed to his chest. *Verita's warning me,* he thought.

He added: "Truth versus feeling?"

A pause. Then her answer:

"Truth steady foundation. Feelings change."

Fidel's fingers tightened on the handle. *That's what Verita always is—steady. Unshaken.*

He added one more signal:

"Miss you deeply."

*Not just your presence,* he thought. *Your voice. Your clarity.*

Her light returned:

"Wait faithful." "Heart connected."

He exhaled slowly. *She's anchoring me to truth. I'm anchored to Verita.*

\*\*\*

Within days, Metamorphia's influence spread through the village like wildfire. People who had lived their entire lives one way now declared themselves to be something entirely different. A slight young man now proclaimed himself a warrior, donning makeshift armor and adopting an exaggerated swagger. A woman who had struggled with numbers her entire life pronounced herself a mathematical genius, dismissing her previous difficulties as merely the result of others' limitations put on her.

Most striking were those who embraced more extreme transformations. Gavril, the baker's son, now moved on all fours, insisting he had always known himself to be a wolf trapped in human form. Lydia, a grandmother of three, wrapped herself in scaled fabrics and spoke in hisses, while her grandchildren cowered in corners, whispering, "Why won't Grandma hold us anymore?"

"I feel so free," she told anyone who would listen. "For seventy years, I've been forced to live as something I'm not. Now I can finally be my true self."

Fidel observed these changes with growing unease. Yet he could not deny the newfound confidence that radiated from those who had embraced Metamorphia's teachings. People who had once been crippled by self-doubt now spoke with certainty. Those who had been weak seemed suddenly strong. They expressed that they were finally happy. All seemingly good things.

But in doorways, children asked passersby why their fathers no longer answered to their names, and spouses searched empty eyes for traces of the people they had married. The slow, terrible realization spread through the village that people were choosing lies over truth, madness over the unbearable weight of being themselves after five years of crushing disappointment.

***

As spring warmed into early summer, Metamorphia's philosophy took deeper root. "Previous bridges failed because we tried to build them as who we were told to be, not as who we truly are," she declared one evening as the first summer flowers bloomed. "Think about it—Regulus made us conform to impossible standards that crushed our spirits. Sophia trapped us in endless pursuit of perfect understanding that made the bridge too complex to finish. Ritus buried us in empty rituals. Altruia made us servants instead of bridge-crossers. Optimus made us pretend problems didn't exist. But a bridge built by people living authentically in their true identities—free from all these false constraints—that bridge taps into power beyond ordinary human limitation. That bridge becomes an expression of divine truth itself and cannot fail."

Cordus, the village blacksmith who had worked on every failed bridge over the past five years, raised his voice in caution. "But we cannot simply become whatever we imagine ourselves to be. There is reality—"

"Reality is what we make it," Metamorphia interrupted, her voice sharp as a blade. "Your kind of thinking is what holds us back, what keeps us separated from those we love." Her gaze flicked meaningfully toward Fidel, touching on his deepest yearning.

"Those who cannot support your metamorphosis are not truly for you," she continued, addressing the crowd as families quietly shattered around them. "Even if they are family, even if they claim to love you, if they cannot affirm who you truly are, they must be cut off. They are anchors drowning you in the false self."

***

Construction of the new bridge began with a ceremony unlike any before, as early summer bloomed around them. Metamorphia stood at the riverbank, resplendent in garments that seemed to shift and change in the light, her makeup transforming her features into something almost inhuman in its perfect symmetry.

"Today we build not just with wood and stone, but with our authentic selves," she proclaimed. "Each person will contribute as their true identity, not the false one imposed by nature or society."

The workers approached their tasks with fervent energy. Those who identified as giants lifted stones that should have been beyond their strength, some collapsing under weights their bodies could not actually bear. Those who claimed supernatural abilities attempted to move materials through willpower alone, growing frustrated when reality failed to conform to their perceived identity.

Through the expanded Night Watchmen's Code, Fidel and Verita could now share complex observations across the water:

"Bridge begins again." "Workers believe they are changed." "Dangerous thinking spreading."

"Western side watching carefully," she replied.

"Too many failures seen. People afraid to hope."

The revelation that her shore had essentially given up building attempts wasn't lost on him. *After five disasters, they've learned caution,* he realized.

\*\*\*

As summer progressed into late July, the bridge extended farther each day, its construction a strange hybrid of actual work and symbolic gestures. Those transformed into animals would circle the bridge supports, sometimes howling at the stones. Those who identified as ancient sages would mumble invented incantations over joining elements. Those who claimed supernatural identities would gesture dramatically at critical junctures, insisting they were strengthening the bridge through powers only they could access.

When structural issues arose—support beams that couldn't bear weight, foundations that shifted in the riverbed—Metamorphia had a ready explanation.

"These problems only exist because some among us still cling to their old self," she insisted. "If everyone fully embraced their true identities, they would build with unprecedented power and focus."

Those who raised practical concerns found themselves labeled as "deniers" and pushed to the margins of the community. Cordus and other experienced builders were forbidden from the construction site after pointing out fundamental flaws in the design.

"They would rather silence us than hear the truth," Cordus told Fidel as they watched from a distance. "But a bridge does not stand on wishes and declarations."

***

By early autumn, the bridge had achieved something unprecedented—it extended nearly ninety percent of the way across the river, farther than any previous attempt. The gap between the eastern structure and the distant western shore had narrowed to perhaps thirty feet, close enough that voices could carry across the water.

Excitement in the village reached fever pitch. After five years of devastating failures, they were tantalizingly close to success. Metamorphia's followers proclaimed that their authentic self-expression had conquered where all others had failed.

"Tomorrow," Metamorphia announced as sunset painted the nearly-complete span with golden light, "we will make the final push. Our true selves will span the entire gap. We will reach them, and show them the power of living as who we truly are!"

That night, Fidel raised his lantern with trembling hands:

"Bridge nearly complete." "Tomorrow final crossing." "See you soon?"

Across the river, her reply came after a pause:

"Something feels wrong." "Watch for danger signs."

*She feels it too,* Fidel thought. *Something's off.*

"Ninety percent finished." "Closest ever achieved."

Her response chilled him:

"Closer to disaster." "Greater the height." "Harder the fall."

***

Dawn broke with an unseasonable chill as villagers gathered for what they believed would be their triumph. The bridge, a chaotic collection of styles reflecting the disparate "identities" of its builders, stretched across most of the water toward the empty western shore.

Metamorphia stood at the eastern edge, more transformed than ever. Her appearance had grown increasingly extreme over the months; her hair an unnatural shade, her features contoured beyond human proportions, her clothing a dramatic statement of her constructed identity.

"Today," she announced, "we prove that authentic self-expression conquers all barriers. When we cross this bridge as who we truly are—we achieve what all others failed to accomplish."

The procession began with drums and banners, each person stepping onto the bridge in elaborate costumes celebrating their chosen identities. Gavril on all fours, Lydia in her serpent persona, dozens of others in their transformed states.

They had reached perhaps three-quarters of the way across—farther than anyone had ever traveled over the river—when Cordus appeared at the shore, shouting desperately.

"The foundation stones!" he cried, pointing toward the water. "Look at the supporting connections."

Those still on shore felt the bridge shudder beneath the procession's weight. Cordus, whose experienced eye could read structural stress in the bridge's movement, saw the subtle but telltale signs—the way certain joints flexed beyond their limits, how the entire span swayed with a rhythm that spoke of fundamental instability.

"The stress points!" he cried, pointing toward the bridge. "Look at the way it's moving!" The bridge's overextension, combined with the chaotic construction methods, had created stresses the foundation could not bear.

"Come back!" Fidel shouted toward the bridge. "It's not stable!"

But Metamorphia, leading the procession near the bridge's end, turned with fury in her eyes. "Deniers!" she screamed back. "You cannot accept our success! Your negativity threatens our achievement!"

She gestured dramatically toward the remaining gap. "We are almost there! Our authenticity will carry us the final distance!"

The center section gave way with a sound like thunder. Unlike the swift, decisive failures they had witnessed before, this disaster unfolded in horrifying slow motion. The overextended bridge twisted as it fell, sections breaking apart in sequence, throwing dozens of people into the churning waters below.

Fidel watched in horror as the procession of transformed villagers plummeted toward the river. As they fell, their constructed identities seemed to dissolve—elaborate makeup washing away, costumes tearing to reveal ordinary clothes beneath, the masks of transformation literally falling away to reveal frightened human faces.

Timidia was among the first to fall, her expression one of utter disbelief as reality finally asserted itself. For a brief moment, as she plummeted, Fidel glimpsed not Metamorphia the confident transformer, but Timidia the frightened girl who had never recovered from being overlooked in her grief.

The rescue effort continued through the day and night. Twenty-nine confirmed dead, nearly forty injured—a catastrophic toll that dwarfed the single death from Regulus's bridge by an unthinkable magnitude.

***

As autumn deepened and the village counted its devastating losses, the psychological impact was unlike anything they had experienced. Previous failures had been disappointing; this had been catastrophic. Families were shattered, not just by death but by the realization that they had been living elaborate lies.

Those who survived the collapse found themselves adrift, no longer certain who they really were. The confident identities they had constructed lay as broken as the bridge itself.

In the days following the collapse, Fidel found himself moving through the village like a shepherd among scattered sheep. Unlike previous failures, this disaster had shattered something fundamental—not just hope, but people's sense of reality itself.

Throughout the village, Fidel found others trapped in despair. A young man who had proclaimed himself a warrior now sat paralyzed by shame, unable to face his family. A woman who had embraced an elaborate false identity couldn't remember how to be herself again. An elderly man who had spouted invented wisdom now questioned everything he'd ever believed.

Rather than trying to fix everyone, Fidel learned to listen—really listen—to what lay beneath their confusion. Most weren't grieving their false identities; they were grieving the hope those identities had represented.

"I wasn't really a sage," admitted one man who had spouted invented wisdom. "But for a few months, I felt important. Like I mattered."

"You do matter," Fidel replied. "Not because of what you pretended to be, but because of who you actually are. A father who loves his children. A neighbor who helps others. That was never false."

When violent arguments broke out between survivors and families of the dead, Fidel found himself mediating—not by taking sides, but by helping each group hear the others' pain. When despair threatened to turn into mob violence against Metamorphia's remaining followers, he stood between them, absorbing anger until it exhausted itself.

Most importantly, he learned to hold hope steady when others couldn't. Not false optimism, but the quiet certainty that even the worst disasters eventually ended, that communities could heal, that love persisted even through profound loss.

"How do you keep going?" asked Harmonia one evening as they worked together to organize meal distribution for families too broken to care for themselves.

"Someone has to hold the center," Fidel replied, surprising himself with the words. "When everything falls apart, someone has to remember that people can be put back together."

***

"We have to face the truth," Cordus said during one of the village meetings, his voice heavy with grief. "Six attempts. Six failures. Maybe we're not meant to cross this river. Maybe some separations are permanent."

Nods of bitter agreement rippled through the gathered survivors. The accumulated weight of six disasters had finally broken something fundamental in the community's spirit.

"No more," declared an elder whose grandson had died in the collapse. "No more builders. No more promises. No more false hope. We bury our dead and learn to live with what we've lost."

The sentiment spread like a contagion of despair. After six years of repeated trauma, the village had reached its breaking point. Anyone who spoke of future bridges was shouted down. Anyone who suggested another attempt was driven away.

The community that had once welcomed every new builder with desperate hope now viewed all such figures with suspicion and hostility. They had learned, through devastating experience, that hope itself could be a weapon turned against them.

***

That night, as the first winter winds began to blow across the empty bridge site, Fidel raised his lantern with hands that shook from more than cold.

"Sixth failure complete." "Twenty-nine dead this time." "Village broken beyond repair."

Across the river, Verita's light appeared after a long pause:

"Truth always surfaces." "False masks eventually fall."

"Community refuses more attempts." "All hope abandoned now." "No future builders welcome."

Her response came slowly:

"Deepest darkness comes." "Before final dawn." "Truth will find way."

Fidel stared across the water, his heart heavy with accumulated grief. *Six attempts. Six disasters. And still she believes.*

"Love beyond everything," he signaled, the familiar arc trembling in his grasp.

"Heart forever yours," came her steady reply.

"Wait faithful together."

As he lowered his lantern, Fidel realized that Metamorphia's disaster had accomplished something no previous failure had achieved—it had convinced the community that the river was uncrossable, that all builders were deceivers, that hope itself was a cruel delusion.

The community that had once welcomed every new builder with desperate hope now viewed all such figures with suspicion and hostility. Six years of repeated trauma had taught them that hope was a luxury they could no longer afford. The very idea of another bridge attempt became taboo, spoken of only in whispers and met with bitter laughter.

In the growing darkness, only two lights still found each other across the void—a faithful love that no disaster could destroy, a connection that persisted despite every reason to despair. Whatever lay ahead, this simple exchange of light in the darkness remained unbroken, untainted by the failures that surrounded it.

# CHAPTER TEN

## *Hope Deferred*

### MAKES THE HEART SICK

"I identify as Verita," she said—her voice calm, her form familiar... and not.

Fidel stumbled backward, clutching his lantern, blinking hard. "No," he said, voice hoarse. "Verita is across the river. I've been signaling to her every night—for nearly six years."

The figure took a step closer, hand extended. "Are you certain?" she asked softly. "Perhaps what you want to believe has blinded you to the truth." The distance between them vanished. Suddenly, impossibly, she was there—close enough to touch. Her breath warmed his neck. Her fingers brushed his hand, sending a jolt through him.

She looked into his eyes. Eyes that matched Verita's. That saw into him like no one else ever had.

He didn't move. Could it be?

Her hand rose to his chest, resting just over his heart. A familiar pressure. A warmth he hadn't felt in years. "I waited," she whispered. "But I crossed." The words melted into his skin. Her other hand slid up to cup his face, pulling him gently toward her. Their foreheads touched. Then her lips hovered over his—near enough to steal his breath.

Every part of him ached to close the final distance. But something held him back. The weight in his pocket. The carved wooden bird. The real Verita's gift. His eyes opened wider. He pulled back.

"You're not her."

*He lifted his lantern and its light spilled across her features—almost perfect. Almost.*

*The illusion cracked. Her expression shifted from tenderness to something darker. "So certain," she said. "So faithful to a phantom." And then she vanished into mist.*

Fidel woke with a jolt, breath ragged, the morning light just beginning to edge over the hills. The lantern was still beside him. The night had passed. The figure was gone.

Just a dream.

But the longing remained, clinging to his chest like a fading scent.

***

Six months had passed since then, and now the effects of six years of repeated failure had become unbearably apparent.

"Hope deferred makes the heart sick," muttered Elder Pax, his once-clear eyes now clouded with cataracts and despair. He sat alone on the crumbling steps of what had once been the village meeting hall, rocking slightly, the same phrase escaping his lips every few moments like an involuntary tick. Few bothered to listen anymore. At twenty-eight, Fidel had heard those words so many times they had become part of the village's rhythm, like the tolling of a funeral bell that never stopped.

The river bore the scars of six failed attempts, each leaving its own distinctive mark. Regulus's perfect stones lay scattered in jagged heaps, their precise angles now mocking in their brokenness. Sophia's elegant curves had been abandoned mid-construction, the unfinished span jutting uselessly into the water like a scholar's half-formed thought. Ritus's three ornate monuments still stood in the rushing current—beautiful, carved with sacred texts, completely useless—permanent reminders of ceremony that had devoured its own purpose.

In the distance, Altruia's bridge platforms remained active, still serving as a floating community where people fed the hungry and healed the sick, but the span itself reached only two-thirds across—forever trapping its workers in endless service instead of enabling them to reach the other shore. The condemned remains of Optimus's bridge swayed visibly in the wind, close enough to completion to mock their hopes but too dangerous for anyone to cross. And scattered throughout the water, the newest additions to this graveyard were the chaotic remains of Metamorphia's span—twisted sections that had torn themselves apart, still occasionally shifting as pieces broke free to be carried downstream.

The village itself had become an extension of this wreckage. Gardens once tended with pride now overflowed with weeds that grew taller each year. Homes sagged with neglect, their owners seeing little purpose in repairs when each day brought the same crushing weight of separation. The communal spaces, once vibrant with shared meals and celebrations, stood empty save for those who sought dark corners to nurse their private sorrows.

Fidel walked through streets he barely recognized, past people who had become strangers. At twenty-eight, he moved with the weight of a much older man, his broad shoulders bowed by years of watching hope die repeatedly.

Garus, once the village's master stonemason, now spent his days in drunken oblivion behind the tavern, bottles scattered around him like the stones he once shaped with loving precision. His face bore the hollow look of a man who had watched six attempts fail in six different ways.

"Another day in paradise," Garus slurred, raising a half-empty bottle in mock salute. "Another day of not seeing my wife and daughters. Over six years now. Six!" He held up trembling fingers. "Can't remember their faces anymore. Isn't that funny? I used to know every freckle on my little one's nose. She'd be fifteen now. Fifteen. Doesn't even know her father's alive."

Nearby, two brothers who had once worked side by side now stood nose-to-nose, shouting in each other's faces, their argument visible even from a distance. These same two had fought over every failed attempt—supporting different approaches, blaming each other for the disasters that followed.

"You supported every single one of them!" the older one screamed, spittle flying. "Perfect law that crushed us! Endless philosophy that went nowhere! Empty rituals that became monuments! Service that trapped people forever! Positive thinking that ignored reality! And transformation that killed twenty-nine people!"

"And what about you?" the younger countered, his voice cracking with six years of suppressed rage. "You stood with Regulus when he called us unworthy! You chanted with Ritus while the bridge became decoration! You believed Optimus when he told us to ignore the cracks! You've endorsed every lie for six years!"

The argument devolved into a brawl, neither brother noticing the small child watching from the shadows, tears running silently down her dirty face—a child who had known nothing but division her entire life.

No one intervened. Public fighting had become as common as breathing, barely worthy of notice. The weight of accumulated grief had crushed the community's capacity for empathy. Six failures had taught them that intervention only led to disappointment.

***

In the remains of what had once been the village council chamber, a handful of elders sat in dispirited silence. Their role as leaders had been rendered meaningless by repeated failure. Who would follow those who had endorsed six catastrophes? Who would trust their judgment after watching them celebrate each new savior, only to bury the bodies when hope turned to horror?

"We should consider... controlled separation," suggested Elder Pax, his voice barely audible. His hair had gone completely white in the six years since the original collapse. "Accept that the divide is permanent. Begin the process of forgetting."

"Forgetting?" Elder Moriah's voice cracked. His granddaughter, born just before the collapse, was now six years old—a child he had never held. "I have family on the other side. Children, grandchildren I've never been able to hold. You suggest I 'forget' them?"

"Better that than this slow death," Pax replied, gesturing toward the window where another funeral procession passed. "How many more suicides must we endure? Eight this month alone."

"Nine," corrected Elder Moriah flatly. "Mira threw herself from the eastern cliff at dawn. Left four children behind." He paused, consulting a scroll. "That makes nineteen confirmed suicides since the first collapse. Not counting the ones who simply... wandered into the wilderness."

The news landed without shock. Suicide had become so commonplace that it registered only as a statistical update, not tragedy. They kept records now, like a harvest count or tax collection—the bureaucracy of despair.

"The pattern is clear," Elder Pax continued, his voice hollow with recognition. "Perfect standards condemn us all as failures. Endless learning traps us in theory without action. Sacred traditions become empty performance. Selfless service becomes its own prison. Positive thinking blinds us to real danger. And personal transformation..." He shuddered, remembering the twenty-nine who had died when Metamorphia's bridge tore itself apart. "Personal transformation turned our deepest pain into our greatest catastrophe."

Outside, a group of young people engaged in behaviors that would have scandalized the village six years ago. Now, their reckless abandon and moral deterioration went unremarked. When hope dies slowly over years, restraint and virtue follow.

"Why not?" a young woman laughed bitterly, accepting a vial of bitter herbs that would temporarily erase her pain. She had been twelve when the bridge fell—had grown up knowing nothing but separation and failed promises. "Nothing's ever going to change. Might as well feel good for a few hours." That concoction had taken several lives, but no one seemed to care as hopelessness permeated their lives like smoke from a fire that never stopped burning.

***

Fidel made his way to his signaling point at the riverbank, the wooden bird carving from Verita clutched so tightly in his palm that its features had begun to smooth away. The path was worn deeper now—six years of nightly pilgrimages had carved a groove in the earth, just as the ritual had carved grooves in his soul. Night after night, he had maintained their connection across the river, their signal exchange the only thing keeping him tethered to sanity.

But tonight, even this felt hollow. At twenty-eight, he moved with the careful precision of a man who had learned that hope was dangerous, that each night's successful contact only set him up for the next night's potential devastation.

He raised his lantern, tracing the familiar arc—

"Love."

Across the darkness, the answering light appeared. But something was different. Slower. Dimmer. He could see it now—what six years of watching for salvation had trained his eyes to notice. Her light wasn't just delayed; it was weaker, as if the effort cost her more each night.

He added a sequence they had developed—

"Still here? Wait faithful."

A long pause. Longer than usual. Long enough for Fidel's heart to stop, start, stop again.

Then the signal.

"Barely. Strength fading."

Fidel froze, staring at the distant light. She had never admitted weakness before. Not in six years. Not once. *You were the strong one,* he thought. *You were my anchor. My constant.* At twenty-five, Verita had endured everything he had, watched the same string of failures from her shore. *If you're starting to slip...*

His mind reeled, replaying the last few months. Had her signals grown shorter? Her timing more delayed? Had she been dimming while I was too consumed by my own ache to see it?

He signaled again using their expanded vocabulary:

"Talk deeper. Share burden. Not alone."

Her answer came after another pause:

"River took children. Holding hands. Gone beneath."

Fidel's stomach turned. *They jumped? Holding hands... hoping to reach their parents?* He had heard rumors of such things—children so desperate to reunite with family that they attempted to swim the violent currents. Six years of watching adults fail had driven some of the young to try impossible solutions.

He raised his lantern again, hurriedly:

"Not you. Promise stay. Need you."

A beat. Then her reply:

"Tempting join them. Pain constant. Six years heavy."

He lowered the lantern, chest tightening. He'd thought of it too. More than once, especially after the sixth failure. Let the current carry him across. To her—or to peace. Either way, the ache would end. Six years was a long time to carry hope that felt heavier each day.

He steadied his hand:

"Promise together. Sacred vow. Remember wedding planned."

Her light returned:

"Remember everything. Heart holds you. But weight crushes."

The signals hit hard. He whispered to the night: *Even love becomes weight when it cannot cross over to be with the one it loves.* Six years of faithful signaling, six years of watching promises to cross over arrive only to crumble, six years of carrying love that had nowhere to go but across an impossible divide.

Still trembling, he added one more:

"Believe possible? Hope remains? Together someday?"

The pause stretched. Longer than any before. Long enough for him to wonder if this was the night the light would never return.

He waited.

Then:

"In Creator and you only hope. Faith. Nothing else."

They continued that night, signal after signal using the full vocabulary they had developed over years of separation. But every word felt thinner. Every reply, a flicker against a storm that had been building for six years.

The light remained. But the strength was fading. On both shores, hope was dying not in dramatic collapse but in slow erosion, like stone worn away by water, drop by persistent drop.

***

Fidel sat alone in his sparse room, the wooden bird resting on his palm. Outside, someone wailed; another notification of loss, another family destroyed. The sound barely registered—it had become the soundtrack of their existence.

He thought of the young bride who had thrown herself into the river that morning, dressed in her wedding gown, unable to face another day separated from her husband. She had been married two weeks before the first bridge fell—had just completed her honeymoon when her husband crossed over for a business trip and never returned. Six years as a wife who had never shared a home with her spouse, never built the life they had planned.

He thought of the father who had walked into the wilderness three days ago, leaving behind a note that read simply: "Cannot be a father from here."

He thought of the children growing up without grandparents, the grandparents aging without seeing their grandchildren, the lovers lying alone night after night, reaching for phantoms across empty beds.

He tried to remember the sound of Verita's voice, really remember it, not just the idea of it. But when he reached for the memory, he found only silence. Six years of lantern signals had somehow erased the music of her speech, replaced her laugh with the mechanical dance of distant light. The truth settled into his bones like winter cold. He was forgetting her even as he fought to reach her. Twenty-five now, she would be a different person than the nineteen-year-old he had known. They both were different—aged by separation, worn by watching hope die repeatedly.

"Hope deferred makes the heart sick," Elder Pax had said. But this was beyond sickness—this was death of the spirit while the body continued its mechanical functions. Six years of deferred hope had made the entire village sick, infected with a despair so deep it had become their new normal.

Fidel placed the wooden bird beside his bed and lay down, not bothering to remove his clothes. Sleep would come or it wouldn't; it hardly mattered. In dreams, he sometimes found momentary relief, imagining himself with Verita. But the waking was always worse for the contrast.

He lay there, staring at the ceiling, but sleep eluded him completely. His thoughts turned to their planned wedding, now a distant memory from another lifetime. They had been so certain of their future, so blissfully unaware of how quickly certainty could shatter. Six years ago, they had been young people planning a life together. Now he was twenty-eight, Verita twenty-five, both worn by watching the world offer salvation only to snatch it away.

"Will it ever end?" he whispered to the darkness. "Creator, have you left us? Could you please help us? Even now?"

No answer came. None was expected. After six failures, even prayer felt hollow.

Restless and unable to find peace, he rose and moved to the window. A plain-looking man walked quietly through the village. He carried no tools, wore no elaborate clothing, displayed no remarkable features that would draw attention. In a community sickened by hope perpetually deferred, he moved unnoticed, his utterly ordinary appearance rendering him invisible to eyes accustomed to seeking salvation in the extraordinary.

Through his window, Fidel glimpsed the man pause directly below, looking up toward him. In the faint moonlight filtering through the clouds, their eyes met for a brief moment—a gaze that seemed to see straight through to Fidel's deepest pain and somehow hold it with infinite compassion. Then the stranger continued on, his destination unknown, his purpose unrevealed. In a village that had learned to fear the arrival of saviors, he passed like a gentle breeze—present but unnoticed, ordinary but somehow carrying the weight of extraordinary purpose.

The seventh year was about to begin.

# CHAPTER ELEVEN

# The Ordinary One

## GESHRIEL'S LIFE

Calla, the old man's daughter, wiped his fevered brow with a rag dampened from their dwindling supply of clean water. The river ran nearby, but no one trusted it anymore—not after all that had fallen into it with each bridge failure.

"I'll try to find more herbs tomorrow," she whispered, knowing there would be none. The eastern slopes had been picked bare years ago.

A shadow darkened the doorway.

"Excuse me," came a voice so ordinary that it almost didn't register. "I heard coughing. May I come in?"

Calla turned, expecting to shoo away some curious villager, but instead found a plainly dressed man carrying a small pouch and a steaming cup. There was nothing remarkable about him; not tall, not short, neither handsome nor ugly, with simple clothes that bore the dust of travel.

"Who are you?" she asked, her voice sharp with suspicion born of too many false hopes.

"My name is Geshriel," he replied, stepping inside without waiting for an invitation. "I have a tea that might help with your father's cough."

Before Calla could protest, he was kneeling beside the old man, supporting his head and holding the cup to his cracked lips. Geshriel's own hands, Calla noticed, bore calluses of recent labor.

"You're new here," she said, not a question. After six years of isolation, every face was known.

Geshriel nodded. "I arrived a few days ago. I've been helping with some repairs—a roof, old Miriam's well, the communal ovens."

He reached into his pouch and extracted a small jar of salve. "For his chest, morning and night. The herbs grow wild on the eastern slope."

With that, he rose to leave.

"Why help us?" Calla called after him. "We have nothing to give in return. We've had nothing for years."

Geshriel paused at the doorway. "Because you needed it," he answered simply, and was gone.

***

As he walked through the village that evening, Fidel noticed a figure working at the abandoned village well; a once-vital source of fresh water that had fallen into disrepair after the fourth bridge failure three years ago. The stranger worked methodically, clearing debris from the well's depths with practiced efficiency.

Curious, Fidel approached. "You're working late."

The man looked up, revealing an utterly forgettable face, but utterly memorable eyes so full of compassion. Fidel paused—this was the same stranger he had glimpsed from his window the night before, the one who had looked up at him with such understanding.

"The moon provides enough light," he replied, his voice as plain as his appearance. "And people need clean water."

"This well has been dry for years," Fidel pointed out. "Since the fourth failure, at least."

"Not dry," the man corrected gently. "Just neglected. The water is still there, hidden beneath the debris." He lowered his bucket again. "I'm Geshriel, by the way."

"Fidel." He offered no more, having learned caution toward newcomers. However, curiosity rose within him about the man's name; he knew from his studies that in the ancient Aramaic tongue of his forefathers, "Gesh" meant "bridge", but what did the "riel" part mean? He made a mental note to find out.

Geshriel gestured to the well. "Would you like a drink? I've just reached the clean water beneath."

Fidel hesitated, considering whether or not to receive a gift from someone he did not know well. "I'm not thirsty."

"Everyone here thirsts," he said simply. "Though not all recognize what they truly thirst for."

"You know nothing about what I thirst for," Fidel countered, his voice carrying the edge of a man who had heard too many empty promises.

"You thirst for reunion with the woman you signal each night," Geshriel replied calmly. "For the life that was taken from you when the bridge fell six years ago."

Fidel stepped back, startled. "How could you know about—"

"If you truly understood who stands before you," Geshriel continued, "you would ask of me, and I would give you water that never runs dry."

"Water that never runs dry?" Fidel's skepticism was evident, hardened by years of disappointment. "I've heard grand promises before; from Regulus six years ago, from Sophia five years ago, from Ritus four years ago, from Altruia three years ago, from Optimus two years ago, from Metamorphia last year. All promised solutions. Most delivered heartbreak."

Geshriel drew up a bucket of clear water, the first the well had yielded in years. "I make no grand promises," he said. "I simply offer what I have to those who need it."

Despite himself, Fidel found his gaze drawn to the glistening water. Geshriel filled a ladle and offered it to him. After a moment's hesitation, Fidel accepted, drinking deeply. The water was startlingly cold and pure, unlike anything he'd tasted since before the failures.

"You're new here," Fidel said finally.

"Yes." Geshriel continued his work. "I arrived about a week ago."

"Why?" The question carried six full years of weariness.

Geshriel paused, looking up at Fidel with eyes that seemed far deeper than his humble appearance suggested. "Because this is where I'm needed."

***

Later that evening, Fidel stared across the river at the flickering light that had become his lifeline. Six years of waiting. Of longing. Of hope carved into light and sustained against all reason.

At twenty-eight, his face bore lines that spoke of endurance rather than age. His broad shoulders, once carried with youthful confidence, now held the weight of years of accumulated disappointment. Yet each night, without fail, he maintained his vigil.

He raised his lantern and traced a single loop—

"Still here?"

From the Western shore, her answer came slowly, cautiously:

"Here but weary beyond measure."

Then a pause—

He signaled back, his own hope fragile but desiring to increase hers:

"New person arrived. Different from others."

There was another pause. Then he added:

"Six years taught us distrust everyone. He's far different."

*Something's different here,* he thought. *A shift I can't yet name after six years of sameness.*

Her reply came, weighted with experience:

"Hope dangerous feeling now. Proceed careful. Always."

He stared into the night and thought, *After six failed attempts... she's right to be wary. We've learned bitter lessons about hope.*

Then one final signal from her:

"Love endures despite pain. Heart yours always."

Their traditional goodbye, worn thin by six years of nightly communion. As constant as the stars, but dimmed by accumulated sorrow.

***

By the following week, whispers about Geshriel had begun to circulate through the village. Unlike the dramatic arrivals of previous would-be bridge builders, his presence had registered gradually, like water slowly seeping into ground parched by years of drought.

"He fixed my door that's been broken since the earthquake," Clara told her neighbor at the communal well, now flowing with clean water for the first time in years. "Didn't ask for anything. Just fixed it and left."

"I found a basket of fresh bread on my step yesterday," replied the neighbor. "My children said a man left it. They ate their first full meal in months. We've been rationing scraps for so long..."

"Six attempts over six years," murmured Elder Moriah, his aged face thoughtful, his hair now completely white from the accumulated stress. "And now this seventh one comes, different from the others. Seven has always been the number of completion."

Subtle changes rippled through the community. Gardens long abandoned showed signs of clearing, as if made new. Homes began to undergo repairs. Most remarkable were the children, playing once more in the streets, their voices a sound so long absent that it startled the adults who heard it.

Fidel observed it all with guarded detachment, the caution of a man who had watched hope die six times. Each night, he faithfully signaled to Verita, reporting these small changes while refusing to name them as hope.

That evening, he raised the lantern:

"Stranger helps everyone. No grand entrance, no banners flying. Fixed old well, treating every person important."

Her reply came, steady:

"Who?"

Fidel replied:

"Quiet worker, no promises made, just labor honest. Different approach, simple presence offered."

A pause from Verita's side.

"Different how? Pattern broken? Hope dangerous?"

Fidel stood still for a moment, watching the light flicker gently across the six-year divide.

He answered:

"Yes different. Unusual. No designs apparent, no promises spoken, just presence steady."

*No designs. No promises. Just presence,* he thought. *Maybe that's what we needed all along, after all these years of grandiose failures.*

***

Later that night, Fidel heard the rare sound of laughter. He followed it, walking through the village streets toward the sound. As he passed near the humble dwellings, he was surprised to see Calla helping her father walk slowly outside their doorway. He moved with careful steps, but his posture was straight and strong.

"Sir," Fidel called softly, "I heard you were unwell."

The old man looked up, his eyes bright and clear. "I was. Coughing so hard I thought my lungs might tear apart. But three days ago, a stranger brought tea and salve." He took a deep breath, demonstrating. "Within hours, the cough began to ease. By this morning, I felt better than I have in years."

Calla smiled, the first genuine smile Fidel had seen from anyone in months. "He wouldn't take payment. Just said his name was Geshriel."

Fidel's pulse quickened. The same man who he had talked with, who had restored the well, now healing the sick with simple remedies.

Before Fidel could reply, that sound drew his attention—that same laughter, closer now. He excused himself and followed the sound, finding himself drawn to the worst section of the village, a collection of hovels where the most broken souls had gathered over the years. To his surprise, he spotted Geshriel sitting among them, sharing a simple meal around a small fire. More surprising still was these broken people were actually laughing.

Fidel moved closer, staying in the shadows. Geshriel wasn't performing miracles or making speeches. He was simply listening as an elderly woman recounted a story from her youth.

"—and then the goat ate my father's best hat!" the woman concluded.

Geshriel's laughter rang out; not polite or measured, but genuine and uninhibited. His ordinary face transformed completely, momentarily radiant with unguarded joy. The others joined in, their own laughter loosened by his abandon.

A man with a badly scarred face—scarred in the third failure, Fidel remembered—suddenly addressed Geshriel directly.

"Why sit with us?" he asked bluntly. "We're the village refuse. The ones they wish would disappear. Years of failures have made us untouchables."

Geshriel's response was matter-of-fact. "I sit with you because you welcome me. And because every person matters, every story matters, especially those most people ignore."

"Even mine?" challenged the woman whose mind had fractured after losing all three children in the sixth bridge attempt. She had been wandering the village edges for years now, speaking to shadows.

"Especially yours, Liora," Geshriel replied, using her name when most had forgotten she had one. "Micah, Esther, and little Samson, they are precious, and their stories live on through you."

The woman's wild eyes filled with tears. "You know their names? After all these years, someone remembers their names?"

"They were brave to try crossing. Their courage should be remembered," Geshriel said, with much love and compassion pouring out.

Fidel retreated into the shadows, disturbed by what he'd witnessed. This was not the theatrical compassion of Altruia or the self-serving kindness of Optimus. This was something else entirely; an ordinary man sitting with the forgotten, speaking of worth and remembrance when six years had taught them all they were worthless.

***

That night, as Fidel walked back to his dwelling, his mind churned with unexpected questions. For many years, his love for Verita had been his north star; constant, unwavering, focused entirely on reunion. But watching Geshriel sit with the forgotten ones stirred something new in him.

He pulled out the wooden bird Verita had carved, its details worn smooth from years of anxious handling. *True love seeks the beloved's good,* he realized, *even when it doesn't align with one's own desires. This was how Geshriel loved; not grasping, not demanding, but giving with open hands.*

Fidel felt as though a narrow passage in his heart had suddenly widened, allowing love to flow more freely. He still longed for Verita with every fiber of his being—years of separation had only deepened that longing—but something was shifting in how he understood that longing.

***

The following day, Fidel was repairing his signaling lantern by the riverbank when he sensed someone approaching. Turning, he found Geshriel standing nearby, watching the churning waters with a thoughtful expression.

"Six attempts," Geshriel said without preamble. "Six failures over six years."

Fidel's hands stilled on the lantern. "You've heard the story, then."

"Parts of it. I'd like to hear your version."

"Why?" Fidel challenged. "Planning to be the seventh failure?"

Geshriel smiled slightly. "I haven't mentioned building any bridge."

"Then why are you here? Everyone comes with a solution, a system, a way across. Six years of the same promises."

"I came because people are suffering," Geshriel replied simply. "The bridge is secondary to that."

Fidel barked a harsh laugh. "Secondary? The bridge is everything. Without it, families remain divided, lovers separated, children orphaned. For all these years we've been cut in half."

Geshriel sat on a nearby rock. "Tell me about her."

The question caught Fidel off guard. "What?"

"The woman you signal to each night. Tell me about her."

For a moment, Fidel considered refusing. But something in Geshriel's straightforward request bypassed his defenses.

"Her name is Verita," he said finally. "We were to be married the day after the bridge collapsed."

"That's her name," Geshriel observed. "I asked about her."

The distinction struck Fidel hard. When had the woman he loved become an abstract goal rather than a living, breathing person? When had years of separation made her more symbol than woman?

"She laughs with her whole body," he found himself saying, memories flooding back. "When something truly amuses her, it's like joy takes physical form. She never lies; not to be kind, not to spare feelings. Her name means 'truth,' and she lives it completely. She would be twenty-five now. A woman, not the nineteen-year-old girl I knew."

"You miss her truth as much as her presence," Geshriel observed.

"Yes." The admission felt wrenched from somewhere deep. "In a world of false hope and pretty lies, she was my anchor to what's real. She's never once lied to spare my feelings."

Geshriel nodded. "And now you signal across darkness, trusting that it's her answering light you see."

"It's her," Fidel said firmly. "We have codes, private signals only we would understand. We've developed an entire language."

"Faith in what you cannot touch," Geshriel remarked. "Interesting."

"Not faith," Fidel corrected. "Knowledge. Nightly proof."

Geshriel smiled again, neither agreeing nor disagreeing. "The others who came before me, tell me about them."

Fidel's expression darkened. "Regulus in the first year with his perfect standards that no one could meet. Sophia in the second year with her perfect knowledge that couldn't translate to reality. Ritus in the third year with his empty ceremonies. Altruia in the fourth year with her service that couldn't sustain itself. Optimus in the fifth year with his self-belief that fed on desperation. Metamorphia in the sixth year with her transformations that denied truth and led to catastrophe." Each name landed like a stone. "Most delivered heartbreak. Two delivered death. Six years of broken dreams and bodies in our river."

"The pattern of six is written throughout creation," Geshriel said, his steady eyes reflecting something timeless. "Six days of creation, mankind was created on the sixth day, six being man's number, God rested on the seventh day. Six wings on the seraphim who guard the throne, six cities of refuge in the ancient laws, six chambers in the honeycomb where sweetness is stored. The seventh always brings rest. The seventh always completes."

"What do you think I'm saying?" Geshriel paused.

The direct question left Fidel momentarily speechless. After so many grandiose claims... "I... don't know," he admitted finally. "You haven't really promised anything."

"No," Geshriel agreed. "I haven't."

\*\*\*

In the square, two factions faced each other with unmistakable hostility. Between them stood a teenage boy, bloodied and trembling. He had been only eight when the bridge fell; had grown up knowing nothing but division.

"He defaced the memorial!" shouted a voice. "Removed his father's name, claiming he 'identifies' as someone with a living parent!"

"His truth is valid!" countered another. "If he experiences his father as alive, who are you to impose your reality?"

The boy, caught between incompatible worldviews that had crystallized over years of separation, looked terrified.

Geshriel moved forward, his ordinary appearance causing him to slip through the crowd unnoticed until he stood beside the boy. He placed a hand on the youth's shoulder.

"What's your name?" he asked quietly.

"Eli," the boy whispered.

"Tell me about your father, Eli."

"He... he died in the collapse," Eli said, his voice breaking. "I was nine. But sometimes, at night, I still feel him sitting on the edge of my bed, like he used to when I had nightmares. Sometimes I hear his voice so clearly." Tears streamed down his face. "Everyone keeps telling me to 'move on,' to 'accept reality.' But what if my reality includes him still being with me somehow?"

Geshriel's response was gentle but clear. "Your father died, Eli. That's the truth, and truth matters. And your experience of his continued love is also real. That matters too."

Confusion rippled through both factions.

"When someone loves you as deeply as your father loved you, that love doesn't simply vanish when they die," Geshriel explained. "Your heart recorded his love for years, and can play back that love at any time. What you're experiencing isn't delusion; it's the heart remembering and feeling his love.

"Accepting that he's gone doesn't mean denying the ways his love still touches you," Geshriel said. "Both truths can exist together."

Something shifted in the crowd; a collective exhale, as if a tension wire pulled too tight for years had finally been released.

A well-dressed merchant approached, his fine clothes marking him as one who had prospered during the years of division. "Teacher, what gives you the right to speak with such authority? What credentials do you possess?"

Geshriel's eyes seemed to look straight through him. "You ask the wrong question. You seek to validate authority through external signs rather than recognizing truth by its fruit." His voice carried clearly across the gathering crowd. "I tell you, the adulterers and outcasts will find healing before you do."

Murmurs of shock rippled through the crowd. The merchant's face reddened. "How dare you! I've followed every law, supported every rebuilding effort, given to charity—"

"And counted every good deed," Geshriel interrupted gently. "You pile up your righteousness like coins, thinking to purchase what cannot be bought. But I tell you, the woman who sells herself for bread yet weeps for her choices will reach wholeness before you do."

Muttering spread through the crowd, some angry, some thoughtful. Fidel watched in growing alarm as several faces hardened with hostility. Several religious leaders pushed forward, their faces dark with anger—men who had built power structures during the years of separation.

"Who are you to speak to us this way?" called a harsh voice from the back. "Coming here with your simple answers, your carpenter's hands, your common face. What do you know of our suffering? Six years we've endured!"

Geshriel's expression remained serene. "I know that true suffering isn't healed by perfect laws, perfect knowledge, perfect rituals, perfect service, perfect belief, or perfect self-creation," he replied. "Those approaches failed because they addressed symptoms while ignoring the disease."

"And what disease is that?" someone challenged.

"The disease of the human heart," Geshriel said, like a healer diagnosing a terminal condition, "the disease of human pride and rebellion, deception, unforgiveness, greed and lust."

Through the shifting bodies, Fidel glimpsed three figures observing from the shadows; their expressions as they watched Geshriel were identical: calculated hatred. Clearly Geshriel was saying things they did not want to hear.

***

That night, as Fidel raised his lantern to signal Verita, his hands trembled slightly.

"New man, simple manner, heals broken. Fixed old well, sat with grieving, touched sick hearts, no pride shown."

Across the river, her light answered:

"Name? Background? Identity certain?"

Fidel hesitated. There was no simple way to communicate it with their expanded signals. He simply responded:

"Bridge. EL suffix" he spelled out the EL with big lantern sweeps.

"Of God" said Verita.

He stared at her signal, heart racing. *EL. God. Yes... the name ends that way.* Then it hit him. *Geshriel. Gesh... bridge. El... God.* His breath caught. "Bridge of God". "Geshriel."

He raised his lantern in one wide sweep,

"Bridge maker. Divine connection."

He stepped back from the edge, the truth rising inside him like dawn breaking across six years of darkness:

*He's not just another helper. He's the bridge of God.*

\*\*\*

As her light dimmed for the night, Fidel turned to find Geshriel standing nearby, watching him with gentle understanding.

"How do you know what we most need?" Fidel asked, his voice low with wonder. "The well, the healing, the truth... after these years of emptiness."

Geshriel's smile deepened, transforming his plain face into something momentarily luminous. "Because I know the heart's true thirst."

"Is it really so simple?" Fidel insisted. "After everything we've tried? After all these failures?"

"Have you tried everything?" Geshriel asked softly. "Or have you only tried building bridges based on human wisdom and effort?"

Before Fidel could respond, shouts erupted from the village, angry voices calling Geshriel's name. The three figures Fidel had noticed earlier had gathered followers, their faces contorted with rage as they approached the riverbank.

"They're coming for you," Fidel warned.

Geshriel nodded calmly. "Yes. They are."

"What will you do?" Fidel asked, surprised by his own sudden concern for this ordinary man who had quietly challenged everything he thought he knew.

Geshriel's response was as simple as his appearance yet somehow contained depths Fidel couldn't fathom. "What I came to do," he said. "Be the Bridge of God."

Earlier that day, Geshriel had quietly approached Fidel as he worked on repairs near the old bridge foundations. "I've been watching you," Geshriel said simply. "The way you examine the failed structures, ask questions about what went wrong. You've learned much over these years."

Fidel paused in his work, surprised. "I've tried to understand each failure. Garus taught me about stone and mortar after Regulus's collapse. I studied Sophia's abandoned blueprints to understand load distribution. Working with Harmonia after Ritus's disaster showed me how to coordinate people through crisis."

"And after the worst disasters?" Geshriel prompted gently.

"Metamorphia's collapse..." Fidel's voice grew heavy. "Twenty-nine dead. I learned that sometimes the most important leadership is simply holding people together when everything falls apart. Helping them process trauma without losing hope entirely."

Geshriel nodded, his eyes reflecting deep understanding. "You've gained exactly what this community will need—not just someone who waited faithfully, but someone who prepared wisely. The reunited shores will need a leader who understands both the technical and human elements of building something that lasts."

"You speak as if the bridge will actually succeed this time," Fidel said quietly.

"It will," Geshriel replied with quiet certainty. "And when it does, these people will need someone who has learned from every failure, who can guide them not just in crossing the divide, but in building a community that won't break apart again." He placed a hand on Fidel's shoulder. "Your years of learning weren't wasted, Fidel. They were preparation."

***

Fidel watched in amazement as Geshriel calmly walked directly toward the approaching mob. Somehow, he slipped right through the crowd, not one person able to lay a hand on him as if it were simply not his time.

# CHAPTER TWELVE

# *The Teacher*

## GESHRIEL'S TEACHING

Six months had passed since Geshriel's quiet arrival at the beginning of the seventh year. Now, at the midpoint of that year—his influence had grown steadily. At twenty-nine, Fidel had learned to recognize hope with caution—six years of repeated failures had taught him that much. Yet something about this teacher felt different from all who had come before.

A small crowd had gathered in the natural amphitheater formed by ancient trees. A woman had approached Geshriel with a question about her withered garden, and he was using a handful of soil to explain principles of renewal and patience.

"Even ground that appears dead still holds life," Geshriel said, allowing the dark earth to sift through his fingers.

The woman's skeptical expression gradually softened as he spoke. "But we've tried everything. Nothing grows in soil that's been neglected for seven years, even hope itself seems to have died."

Geshriel smiled gently. "Have you noticed the wildflowers along the river's edge? They grow most abundantly where the wreckage of failed bridges has fallen."

"What does that mean?" she pressed.

"That life often finds its strongest expression in places of greatest brokenness."

A man clutching a crude walking stick rose from where he'd been sitting among the gathered listeners. "Pretty words. But they don't fill empty stomachs or rebuild broken families. Six years of pretty words from six different failures."

Geshriel studied him without defensiveness, his gaze taking in the man's face marked by years of wind and sun, and the pain etched in his posture. "Jaris, isn't it? The carpenter who lost his daughter in the sixth attempt?"

The man stiffened, surprised at being known. "What of it? She'd be twenty-two now. A woman grown, with children of her own perhaps, if she'd lived."

"Nothing grows from soil that remains closed," Geshriel said kindly. "Not crops, not bridges, not healing."

"Are you suggesting my grief is a choice?" Jaris demanded, his voice rising. Several in the gathering shifted uncomfortably, anticipating one of the angry outbursts that had become common in the village after years of crushing disappointment.

Geshriel's response held no judgment. "No. Your grief is real and honored. But the wall you've built around it—that was a choice. A necessary one at the time, perhaps, but walls that protect can also imprison."

Jaris's indignation faltered, his eyes suddenly wet. "How else does one survive such loss? Followed by six years of watching hope die again and again?"

"That," Geshriel said, "is one of the questions I came to answer."

He rose from the log and placed his hand gently on Jaris's shoulder, his eyes reflecting a depth of understanding that transcended his common appearance.

"When you build walls to protect your grief, you keep out not just the pain, but also the healing. True survival isn't about isolation, but transformation. The wound doesn't disappear; it becomes a doorway."

Geshriel's voice softened further. "Your daughter's life was a gift, Jaris. And gifts are meant to be shared, not locked away where no one can touch them."

Tears flowed freely down Jaris's face now. "But sharing the memory hurts too much."

"Yes," Geshriel nodded. "At first, it's like reopening the wound. But then something remarkable happens—others help carry what you cannot bear alone. Your daughter's story, her laugh, her kindness; these things were never meant to be imprisoned behind walls of protection, but to continue living through you, as you share with others."

He gestured toward the community gathered around them. "Look at these faces. Each person here carries losses from seven years of separation. When you share yours, and they share theirs, something new is created; a bridge across the deepest divides."

Jaris wiped his eyes with trembling hands. "I...I don't know how to begin tearing down these walls."

"You already are," Geshriel said with a gentle smile. "By asking the question. The rest will come one stone at a time, one memory shared, one moment of connection. And I tell you this; on the other side of that fallen wall, you won't find only pain. You'll rediscover joy."

From the edge of the gathering, a figure stumbled forward—Garus, the stonemason, clutching a half-empty bottle. His weathered face bore the marks of six years of drowning his pain.

"You say walls imprison," Garus called out, his words slurred but his eyes suddenly clear. "What about the wall I built from this?" He held up the bottle, liquid sloshing. "Six years of trying to forget my wife, my daughters. Trying to numb the ache."

Geshriel's gaze met his with infinite compassion. "And has it worked, Garus?"

The stonemason's hand trembled. "No. It's just...stolen more time. More memories." He looked at the bottle, then at the faces around him. "Better to throw away my drink than to throw away my life."

With deliberate motion, Garus poured the contents onto the ground, saying, "If there's hope...if love really can bridge what's been broken.." His voice broke. "I want to remember their faces again."

***

As the weeks passed into early autumn, children gathered around Geshriel regularly in the village square. The afternoon teaching sessions had become a cherished routine. They asked why the river couldn't be easily crossed. Geshriel didn't lecture on physics or engineering. Instead, he picked up a stick and drew in the dirt.

"See this line?" he said, drawing a deep furrow. "Imagine it's the river. Now, if I want to reach the other side,"—he placed a pebble on one side,—"what's the simplest way across?"

The children offered various solutions: jumping, flying like a bird, swimming.

Geshriel nodded. "All good answers. But," he added, gathering some stones and twigs, "let's build something together." He arranged larger stones in a semi-circle around him. The children eagerly joined in, collecting more materials.

"See how each stone by itself can't cross the gap?" Geshriel placed a stone that fell short of spanning between two points. "And how these twigs alone are too fragile?" He demonstrated as a twig bent and broke under minimal weight.

The children nodded, watching intently.

"But what happens when we work together, combining different strengths?" He guided them in creating a simple arch with stones supporting each other, with twigs woven between for stability.

A young girl examined their creation carefully. "The stones hold each other up!"

"And the twigs fill the spaces," added a boy, running his finger along the woven sections.

"What would happen if one stone decided it didn't need the others?" Geshriel asked, gently loosening one of the supporting stones.

The children watched as the structure wobbled. "It would fall!" they chorused.

"And if the twigs said they were too small to matter?"

"There would be holes!" said the girl. "Things would fall through!"

Geshriel smiled, setting the stone back in place. "What does this teach us?"

The children pondered for a moment. Then the boy's eyes lit up. "Nobody's too small or too big! Everyone has a job!"

Fidel, who had been watching from the edge of the gathering, stepped closer. "So the bridge isn't just about materials..."

"What is it about?" Geshriel asked him gently.

Fidel studied the children's creation, understanding dawning in his eyes. "It's about each piece finding where it belongs to help the others."

"And when that happens?" Geshriel prompted.

"What seemed impossible becomes..." Fidel paused, looking at the sturdy little arch, "...inevitable."

Demas, one of the younger followers who had joined them early in Geshriel's ministry, leaned forward eagerly. "When will we begin the actual construction? Surely we could start building immediately."

Geshriel turned to the children's arch. "What would happen if we tried to build this before gathering the right stones?"

"It wouldn't work," said the girl. "You need stones that fit together."

"And if we rushed and didn't let each piece find its proper place?"

"It would collapse," the boy added solemnly.

Geshriel looked back at Demas with gentle patience. "The stones are still being gathered, Demas. And each must be prepared for its place."

***

On one particular afternoon in mid-autumn, Geshriel had drawn his largest crowd yet to the village square. They gathered around the stone memorial bearing names of those lost in the bridge disasters—a somber reminder of their repeated failures over six long years.

Geshriel studied the memorial as he spoke to the assembled crowd. "You've been taught that division is natural, that separation is inevitable. But I tell you that unity is your original state, and division is the aberration."

A skeptic in the crowd called out, "Pretty sentiment, but the river still stands between us and our loved ones. Seven years of pretty sentiments haven't changed that reality."

"Reality," Geshriel replied, "is more than what your eyes perceive or your hands touch. The deepest realities often remain unseen."

"Like what?" challenged another voice.

"Like love," Geshriel answered simply. "Can you see it? Weigh it? Measure it with instruments? Yet who among you would deny its reality?" His gaze swept the crowd before settling on Fidel. "Fidel signals across darkness every night to the one he cannot reach, cannot touch, cannot hold. Is that connection any less real because it transcends physical barriers? For seven years, he has maintained that faith."

Fidel felt the weight of Geshriel's words like a physical pressure against his chest. Each night, he faithfully signaled to Verita, their coded messages a lifeline that had sustained him through seven years of separation. Their vocabulary had grown rich and complex over the years, allowing real conversations across the impossible divide.

A young merchant stepped forward, his fine clothes marking him as one who had prospered during the years of division. "Teacher, you speak of unity, but some of us have worked hard to build what we have. Should those who have succeeded be reduced to the level of those who have failed?"

Geshriel looked at him with such love. "Tell me, in these six attempts to rebuild, what did each builder ask of you?"

The merchant shifted uncomfortably. "Materials, labor, payment for supplies..."

"And what did you ask of them?"

"Premium prices, exclusive contracts, payment in advance even if the bridge failed..."

Geshriel's gaze swept the crowd. "What about the rest of you? In each attempt, what were you seeking?"

A woman called out, "Security for our families."

"Proof that this time would be different," added a third.

Geshriel nodded slowly. "So each builder took what they needed, and each of you took what you wanted. In all this taking, who was giving?"

An uncomfortable silence fell over the crowd.

"The river," whispered a child from the front, her young voice carrying clearly in the stillness.

"The river?" Geshriel asked gently.

"It kept giving us chances. Six times."

Geshriel smiled at her with infinite tenderness. "Yes, little one. And what does a river do when it gives?"

"It flows," she said, then paused, thinking. "It doesn't keep anything for itself. It just keeps giving water."

"From the mouth of children," Geshriel said, his voice carrying to every corner of the amphitheater. "The river teaches what you've forgotten—that true strength flows from giving, not taking."

Fidel noticed several merchants shift uncomfortably at the edges of the gathering. Since the bridge's collapse seven years ago, they had established lucrative monopolies on goods from their side of the river, charging extortionate prices for items once commonly traded. The artificial scarcity created by the division had made them wealthy beyond measure. There were whispers that some had actively sabotaged rebuilding efforts over the years, paying laborers to use faulty materials or miscalculate measurements.

"You've been taught to love friends and hate enemies," Geshriel pressed on. "But I tell you, love your enemies. Pray for those who have harmed you."

"That's madness!" someone objected. "The people who sabotaged our bridges, who profit from our division; we should love them? After seven years of their exploitation?"

"If you love only those who love you, what reward will you get?" Geshriel countered. "Even the most corrupt do that. If you greet only your brothers and sisters, what are you doing more than others?"

He gestured toward the ruined bridge pilings visible in the river. "Six attempts, six failures over six years. None remain to transport you across because none addressed the true division."

"And what is that?" asked an elder, his voice weary with years of disappointment.

Geshriel's reply was direct and unflinching. "The selfishness in your own hearts. The pride that refuses to admit need. The greed that hoards while neighbors starve. The hatred that poisons your souls more than any enemy could. You cannot build unity with hands stained by division, hearts hardened by bitterness, minds clouded by self-righteousness."

An uncomfortable silence fell over the crowd as his words struck home.

As the crowd began to murmur and disperse, Geshriel noticed a group of children attempting to cross a narrow stream. They had laid smooth rocks as stepping stones, but the gaps were too wide for their small strides.

He approached and, without a word, moved the stones closer together. The children crossed easily, then looked back at him with curious eyes. He had built a bridge.

Fidel, who had been following at a distance, found this simple act more compelling than any grand speech. "You speak in riddles," he observed when the children had gone.

Geshriel smiled slightly. "Not riddles. Parables. Stories that hide meaning from some while revealing it to others."

"And which am I?" Fidel challenged.

"That," Geshriel replied, "depends on whether you're asking to understand, or merely to debate."

***

As the winter months approached, Geshriel's influence grew, as did resistance to his teachings. Those who had established power in the fractured community, self-appointed leaders of various factions who benefited from continued division, began to watch him with increasing hostility. Seven years of separation had created entrenched interests that viewed any change as a threat.

On this day in early winter, word had spread that Geshriel would be teaching at the large outdoor amphitheater on the hillside above the village. People arrived from outlying farms and even neighboring communities, hungry for hope, for healing, for any teaching that might break the cycle of despair that had claimed their region since the bridge's collapse seven years ago, and every bridge failure since then merely added to it.

The natural amphitheater buzzed with hundreds of voices as Geshriel took his place on a large stone that served as a speaking platform. A religious leader from a neighboring village stepped forward, his ornate robes drawing attention.

"Teacher," he called out, his voice carrying across the crowd, "by what right do you overturn the teachings of our ancestors? What credentials do you possess to contradict established wisdom?"

Geshriel met his challenge calmly. "Tell me, what did your ancestors teach about love?"

"To love those who deserve it," the man replied confidently. "To reward virtue and punish vice."

"And how has that wisdom served you?" Geshriel asked gently. "Has it built bridges or walls?"

The man sputtered, unprepared for the redirect. Geshriel continued, "I tell you, a tree is known by its fruit. If the fruit of your wisdom is seven years of division and despair, perhaps it's time to examine the roots."

Magistra Theoria stepped forward from the crowd, her scholarly attire reminiscent of Sophia. She had grown wealthy over the past years teaching theories about why reunification was impossible, her "Division Studies Academy" profiting from the separation.

"These teachings contradict established wisdom," she declared. "Seven years of careful study have proven that division is inevitable. The teachings defy rational analysis."

"Human wisdom," Geshriel replied gently, "sees through a glass darkly. What appears contradictory in limited vision becomes coherent when seen from above."

"You speak as if you have such vision," she accused.

"I speak what I know," he answered simply.

As the confrontation intensified, Fidel noticed Councilor Septus at the edge of the crowd. He had risen to power after the bridge collapse by promising "security through separation." Over the seven year period since the first bridge collapse, his border authority had employed guards to prevent desperate families from attempting fatal crossings, while collecting steep taxes for "protective surveillance" along the shore. This empire of fear thrived on preventing reunification, as division sustained his influence and wealth.

The crowd grew restless, with many adversaries speaking loudly and clearly against Geshriel.

Geshriel raised his hand for silence. "You seek to silence me because my words expose what you wish to keep hidden," he said, "like light exposing what is in darkness. But what has been whispered in dark corners will be proclaimed from rooftops."

His gaze found Fidel in the crowd. "The time is coming when this corrupt system will be overturned. Those who profit from division will resist with violence. The bridge you seek cannot be built without sacrifice."

As the hostile factions withdrew, murmuring among themselves, Geshriel continued answering questions from those who remained in the amphitheater.

Fidel approached him after most had departed. "You've made powerful enemies today."

Geshriel nodded. "It was inevitable. Light exposes what darkness hides. People fight the light because it reveals truths they've long buried."

"They could harm you," Fidel warned.

"They will."

"And you'll let them?"

Geshriel looked toward the fractured chasm, his voice low. "The breach runs deeper than stone. To mend it, something more than stone must be laid down."

"What does that mean?" asked Fidel.

Geshriel turned to him, eyes filled with love. "Just remember this: greater love has no one than to lay down his life for his friends. That kind of sacrifice doesn't just repair bridges—it becomes one."

***

That evening, as winter settled over the valley, Geshriel gathered his closest followers in a circle by the riverbank. On the opposite shore, lanterns were being lit, including Verita's distinctive signal to Fidel.

"Go," Geshriel said gently. "Speak to her. Join us when you've finished."

Grateful, Fidel moved to his signaling point and raised his lantern. The familiar pattern of light moved across the divide between them. After seven years, their communication had evolved into sophisticated conversations using the expanded Night Watchman's Code.

He traced a slow arc—

"Love."

Then he signaled using the complex vocabulary they now shared:

"Teacher speaks of sacrifice building bridges."

Across the river, Verita's light answered:

"More details."

Fidel exhaled slowly. He signaled:

"Says cost required. Bridge built inside broken hearts first."

Then:

"Hope remain possible?"

He stared into the darkness. Could it be that their seven-year separation wasn't punishment...but preparation? A refining fire that had strengthened their love beyond what they'd thought possible?

Her reply came gently:

"Soul connection first. Always believed this truth."

Fidel's chest tightened. *From the beginning, she saw through the surface. She always did.*

He responded:

"Fire has made us stronger than before."

Then he paused. Raised the lantern again:

"Miss you desperately after all these years."

Her answer came at once:

"Miss your touch. Dream of reunion nightly."

Fidel closed his eyes. *And yet, Geshriel had said... love must be willing to endure even that absence for the beloved's good.*

He traced another signal:

"Wait worth everything. Love transcends physical distance."

Her response:

"Trust completely. Believe reunion comes through sacrifice."

A pause. Then again:

"Trust fully in this teacher."

No warnings from Verita this time.

Fidel stood there, wind brushing his face, heart heavy but steadier. The pain was still there—but now, it had purpose. Seven years had refined their love into something unshakeable.

When they finally bid goodnight, Fidel returned to the circle where Geshriel was delivering what felt like his most important teaching yet.

"I'm giving you something new," Geshriel was saying, his voice somehow reaching each listener's soul as if whispered just to them. "Let your love for each other mirror the love I've shown you—sacrificial, steady, willing to suffer for the other's benefit. This is how the world will recognize who truly walks with me: not by signs, not by words, but by the way you love."

An older woman spoke up, her face lined with seven years of accumulated loss. "How can we love when love has brought us so much pain? I loved my husband, my children—all lost to the river. Loving again feels like inviting more suffering."

Geshriel's expression held infinite compassion. "Love and suffering are indeed inseparable, but not in the way you think. It isn't that love causes suffering; it's that only love has the power to take your deepest wounds and transform them into doorways through which others find healing. Your pain becomes the very bridge by which someone else crosses from despair to hope."

"How can my family's deaths become a bridge for others?" she challenged, tears streaming unchecked.

"When you choose to comfort another grieving mother instead of nursing bitterness. When you share your husband's wisdom with a confused young man instead of hoarding memories in isolation. When you let your love for lost children overflow to care for the orphaned and forgotten." Geshriel's voice was gentle but firm. "That is how death serves life. That is how love conquers even the grave."

Geshriel continued, looking around the circle, "The bridge you seek cannot be built with mere stone and wood alone. It must be built with living stones; hearts willing to become the bridge."

"What does that mean?" a young man asked. "How can a person become a bridge?"

"When you forgive, reconcile, and love without expectation of return," Geshriel explained, "you build the true bridge." He picked up a handful of gravel. "A bridge of dead stones will always fail. But a bridge built through sacrificial love, that is a bridge the river cannot destroy."

Fidel leaned forward, drawn by words that resonated with something deep within him. "Are you saying the physical bridge is irrelevant?"

"I'm saying the physical bridge is the last step, not the first," Geshriel replied. "First the heart, then the structure. You've been building in reverse order for seven years."

"If we build this heart bridge," a woman asked hesitantly, "will it reunite us with those across the river?"

Geshriel's expression held a shadow of sorrow. "The path to reunion requires sacrifice greater than most imagine. Not ritual sacrifice, not token service, but the laying down of one's very self."

"That sounds like death," someone observed quietly.

"Death and resurrection," Geshriel agreed. "The seed must fall to the ground and die before it produces many seeds. The bridge can only be completed when the builder becomes the cornerstone."

His gaze fixed on Fidel with such intensity that he felt physically warmed by it. "You signal across darkness to one you love. Would you give everything to reach her?"

"Without hesitation," Fidel answered honestly. "Seven years have only deepened that conviction."

Geshriel nodded, a smile of profound understanding crossing his common features. "Remember that," he said quietly. "In the days to come, remember that as you see what they do to me."

A child sitting near the inner circle looked up with wide eyes. "Where did you come from?"

A wistful expression crossed Geshriel's face, his eyes distant with memory.

"I once lived in my father's house," he said softly. "A place of many rooms, filled with light. I helped him with his work from the beginning. I left that home to come here, but I carry it with me always." He touched his heart. "And one day, I will prepare a place for you there."

***

As the winter gathering dispersed into the night, Fidel remained by the riverbank, watching Geshriel gaze toward the distant shore where Verita lived.

"You knew her name," Fidel observed quietly. "You knew about our signals without being told."

Geshriel nodded. "Yes."

"And you know things about people before they speak. You see into hearts like they were open books."

"What do you think that means?" Geshriel asked gently.

Fidel studied this ordinary man who somehow contained such extraordinary wisdom. "I've been watching you for months. You heal with a touch, speak with authority, love with a depth that transforms enemies into friends."

"And what kind of person does such things?"

"I…" Fidel hesitated, the implications staggering. "Only the Creator could know hearts so completely. Only the Creator could love so perfectly."

Geshriel's eyes held infinite patience. "What does your heart tell you?"

Fidel's voice became barely a whisper. "That you're not just a teacher. That you're…" He couldn't finish the words.

"Say it, Fidel."

"You're the Creator. Or his son, aren't you? The Creator's own son."

For just a moment, Geshriel's appearance seemed to shimmer, as if something glorious were contained within his unremarkable exterior. "You've seen truly."

Fidel's knees buckled and he fell forward, clear to the ground, in complete adoration and worship. Gentle hands lifted him.

"Why did you come here?" Fidel asked, his voice shaking. "To this broken place, these broken people?"

"Why do you signal to Verita each night?"

"Because I love her. Because love compels—" Fidel stopped, understanding flooding his face. "You came for love."

"For love," Geshriel confirmed quietly. "And love requires a bridge."

"But surely you could simply command the river to part, or the stones to arrange themselves?"

Geshriel smiled sadly. "Tell me, if I forced your reunion with Verita, removing all choice, all cost, all sacrifice—would your love mean the same?"

Fidel considered this. "No. Love that's compelled isn't love at all."

"So the bridge must be built by love freely given, freely chosen, even unto death," Geshriel's voice itself seemed to brim over with love.

"Death?" The word escaped Fidel like a prayer.

Geshriel's gaze returned to the river, to the broken pilings that marked six years of failure. "The greatest bridges require the greatest sacrifice. And the greatest love…" He paused, his voice heavy with foreknowledge. "The greatest love lays down its life."

Fidel's mind raced, connecting fragments he'd been too afraid to piece together. "The enemies you've made. The threats. You know what they're planning."

"I know."

"And you'll let them?"

"I'll become what this community needs most—not just a teacher, but a foundation stone that connects two sides, and the keystone that can never be moved, never be destroyed." Geshriel turned back to him, his face radiant with purpose. "What you will witness here is how love builds the only bridge that truly lasts."

As winter moved toward its end, and the seventh anniversary of the original collapse approached its climax, the tension in the village grew palpable. Those who opposed Geshriel watched his every move with increasing hostility. But Geshriel continued his work with quiet determination, preparing for something his followers didn't yet understand—something that would transform not just their community, but also the very definition of love itself.

# Chapter Thirteen

# The True Foundation

## Geshriel's Love And Sacrifice

Morning light spilled across the riverbank, illuminating the scars of six failed attempts to bridge the divide. The skeletal remains of previous structures jutted from the churning waters like the bones of fallen giants: monuments to human pride, knowledge, ritual, service, self-belief, and self-creation. All had promised connection. All had delivered only inward focus, division, some death.

Fidel stood at the water's edge, the wooden bird Verita had carved nestled in his palm, worn smooth by a thousand desperate caresses. Seven years of separation had etched patience from his bones. Each night, their signals crossed the void like prayers thrown into an abyss, sustaining a connection that transcended physical barriers yet left his arms achingly empty.

At twenty-nine, Fidel bore the weight of those seven years in every line of his face, in the careful way he moved, as though he carried invisible burdens that had settled deep into his bones.

"You're here early," Geshriel's voice came from behind him, ordinary yet somehow containing depths that defied his unremarkable appearance.

"I couldn't sleep," Fidel admitted, turning to face him. "Your revelation to me of who you are, and your words about building bridges through sacrifice...they followed me into dreams."

Geshriel nodded, his gaze traveling across the river to the western shore. For months, he had taught among them, healing wounds both physical and spiritual, speaking truths that challenged everything they thought they knew. He had spoken of bridges—both across the river and to the Creator—but today they would discuss beginning the actual physical work.

"Walk with me," Geshriel invited, starting along the riverbank.

As they walked, villagers began gathering, drawn by Geshriel's presence. His impact on the community had been profound yet so gradual many hardly realized how much had changed. Once-abandoned gardens now flourished. Repaired homes stood firm. Children played in streets that had known only silence for years. Most remarkably, the poisonous divisions that had defined village life since the bridge collapse had begun to heal.

When a sizable group had assembled, Geshriel led them to a flat area overlooking the river. From this vantage point, all six failed attempts were visible—a perfect classroom for what would come next.

"The time has come," Geshriel announced, his voice carrying to every ear, "to speak directly about building a bridge."

The crowd stirred. Some leaned forward eagerly, while others tensed with the memory of past disasters.

"Six attempts," Geshriel continued, gesturing toward the wreckage. "Six failures. Not because you lacked skill or materials or determination, but because each was built on the wrong foundation."

"What foundation should we use then?" called out a stonemason who had worked on every failed attempt. "We've tried everything!"

"Have you?" Geshriel asked gently. "Regulus built on perfect law, demanding standards no one could meet. Sophia built on perfect knowledge that couldn't translate to reality. Ritus built on empty ceremonies that substituted ritual for relationship. Altruia built on service that turned inward. Optimus built on self-belief that fed on desperation. Metamorphia built on self-creation that denied unchangeable truth." His gaze swept the gathering. "But not one of them built on the only foundation that can span such a divide."

"And what's that?" Fidel asked, though something in him already knew the answer.

"Love," Geshriel replied simply. "More than the feeling, more than the sentiment, but love as action. Love that costs everything. Love that gives itself away."

Elder Moriah shook his head, his voice bitter with experience. "Pretty words. But how does 'love' stack stones or support weight? How does 'love' resist the river's force?"

"By first rebuilding what was broken here," Geshriel answered, placing his hand over his heart. He gestured toward two brothers who had been locked in bitter conflict since supporting different failed approaches. "Before we lay one stone in that river, we must rebuild the bridges between people." He pointed to merchants who had profited from artificial scarcity. "Before we span that water, we must close the gap between those who hoard and those who hunger."

Understanding slowly dawned on faces in the crowd. This was not what they had expected—not another grand construction project, but something both simpler and infinitely more challenging.

"You want us to forgive each other first?" someone asked incredulously. "After everything that's happened?"

"Not just forgive," Geshriel clarified. "Reconcile. Rebuild. Restore. The work begins not in the river but in the village." His eyes found Fidel's. "Will you help me show them?"

Fidel hesitated only a moment before nodding. Whatever Geshriel asked, he would do. This ordinary man with extraordinary wisdom had kindled something in him that felt remarkably like hope.

In the days that followed, Geshriel led them in a different kind of bridge-building. He brought brothers together not for hollow apologies but for genuine conversation about their shared losses. He guided merchants to open their storehouses and establish fair prices, ending the exploitation that had defined commerce since the collapse. He helped families who had aligned with different failed approaches to eat together, pray together, work together.

Most powerful was his work with the outcasts; those deemed worthless or dangerous after the collapse. Under Geshriel's guidance, these forgotten souls became integral to community life again. The woman whose mind had fractured after losing her children found purpose caring for orphaned youngsters. The man whose disfigurement had made him an object of fear became respected for his wisdom rather than shunned for his scars.

Each reconciliation, each restored relationship, each healed division was celebrated as another section of the true bridge under construction. Not of stone or wood, but of human hearts reunited.

Fidel watched it all with growing wonder. Each day he worked alongside Geshriel, and each night he went to the shore to signal Verita.

He raised his lantern and traced the expanded signals they now shared:

"Love growing stronger here," he sent.

"New healing beginning daily."

Across the river, her light responded with measured words:

"Still dark here. Only your signals bring hope."

Fidel's heart ached at her response. While Geshriel's presence had transformed their community, Verita's shore remained trapped in despair.

"Unity building between neighbors. Hearts opening after long bitterness."

Then came her response:

"Miss you desperately still. Always watching for your light. I tell leaders about progress on your side."

Fidel's throat tightened. Even with their expanded ability to share thoughts, he could feel the weight of her isolation. The western shore had no Geshriel to heal their divisions.

"Soon we will stand together again," he signaled.

Her light flashed in reply:

"Pray this time different. Need real hope not just promises."

One morning about two weeks after Geshriel's announcement, he gathered the village at the riverside. "Today," he declared, "we begin the physical work. But not as before."

He led them to a section of shore where the river ran deep and the current strong; precisely where previous attempts had avoided building due to the difficulty.

"We start at the hardest point," Geshriel explained, "not the easiest. We build underwater foundations first, not visible spans that bring quick praise."

When engineers objected that building in such conditions was impossible, Geshriel smiled. "With traditional methods, yes. But we will use a different approach."

He showed them a technique using woven reed baskets filled with a special mixture that hardened underwater instead of dissolving—simple enough for anyone to learn yet ingenious in effect.

"Everyone helps," Geshriel insisted. "The skilled and unskilled, the strong and weak, the old and young."

He assigned tasks based not on ability but on need; those who needed healing in specific ways were given work that would provide exactly that. Those proud of intellect were partnered with the uneducated. Those physically strong worked alongside the frail.

Most remarkably, Geshriel worked harder than anyone—taking on the most demanding roles, lifting what others could not, standing longest in the freezing water. His simple appearance gave no hint of the unshakable strength that sustained him. When asked how he kept going without pause or rest, he would smile and say, "My father's strength flows through me. That is enough."

As work progressed, the community's transformation wasn't without its shadows. Despite Geshriel's teachings about love and sacrifice, old habits died hard. One morning, Fidel noticed a merchant secretly overcharging desperate families for grain. Where his hands had touched the bridge's railing while conducting his dishonest business, an ugly green stain spread across the stone—the color of greed made manifest.

When confronted by workers, he laughed dismissively. "Business is business," he declared, placing his palm firmly on the bridge's surface. The green stain deepened, pulsing like a sickly heartbeat.

Later that same day, two former rivals whispered lies about each other to their respective followers, each claiming the other was sabotaging their shared work. Their hushed conversation took place near the foundation stones, and where their feet stood, inky black stains seeped upward—deception leaving its mark on the sacred structure.

Most troubling was a man who had profited from the years of division by selling false hope to grieving families, claiming he could smuggle messages across the river for exorbitant prices. His exploitation of their desperation was a form of cruel deception, and where his hands touched the bridge, the black stains of dishonesty deepened further—the dark marks of lies told to the vulnerable, promises he never intended to keep.

These stains spread gradually across sections of the bridge, creating a disturbing mosaic of human failing. Workers tried scrubbing them away, but the colors only grew more vivid, as if the bridge itself bore witness to every transgression committed upon its surface.

As days passed, a marvel emerged; the underwater foundation began to take shape, invisible to the eye but detectable through measuring lines. Unlike previous attempts, this structure held firm against the river's force. Something about the materials, the design, the spirit in which it was built, allowed it to withstand what had destroyed all others.

"The foundation stones must be laid in the correct order," Geshriel taught them. "Truth first, then justice, then peace, then love above all. Any other sequence creates instability."

Visible progress remained minimal. Where previous bridge-builders had raised spectacular but ultimately doomed structures, Geshriel's approach created little to admire above water. Some villagers grew impatient, questioning his methods.

"We've been working for weeks," complained one, "with nothing to show for it."

"Nothing?" Geshriel challenged gently. "Look at your hands." The man's hands, once soft from years of idleness, now showed calluses of honest work. "Look at your neighbor." The man turned to the person beside him—someone from an opposing faction he now called friend. "Nothing has changed?"

The man fell silent, understanding dawning.

Fidel worked alongside Geshriel daily, their conversations deepening his understanding of what this extraordinary-ordinary man was truly building. Often Demas joined them, the three working in comfortable rhythm as they shaped foundation stones. Demas proved skilled with his hands, though Fidel noticed he asked fewer questions than the others, seeming content to focus on the physical work rather than Geshriel's deeper teachings about sacrifice and love.

"The bridge is just the visible manifestation," Geshriel explained one afternoon as they shaped foundation stones. "What matters is what it represents—the restoration of what was always meant to be."

"Unity," Fidel offered.

"More than unity," Geshriel corrected. "Communion. Not merely existing side by side but living as parts of one whole."

Each night, Fidel returned to his signaling post, hands steady with purpose.

He lifted the lantern and signaled:

"Foundation growing stronger beneath water. Different approach this time, built on love."

The foundation was unlike anything before—hidden, humble, quiet. Geshriel didn't direct from above; he worked beside the tired, the overlooked, the forgotten.

Across the river, Verita's reply came:

"Your hope reaches across darkness to me. Bridge progress there gives first hope in years."

Fidel paused, then added:

"Builder teaches love must come first before stone. Hearts mended before bridges raised."

Then came unexpected news:

"Your words through signals inspire leaders here. Decided to attempt building again. Started foundation yesterday using reed baskets and special mixture. Like you taught us."

Fidel's heart leaped.

"You're building too? From your side?"

"Yes. Your daily reports of love's foundation gave hope we thought lost forever. Small crew began work. Following same principles you describe."

He stepped back, amazed. Even after seven years of separation, their nightly communication was literally building bridges on both shores.

"Bridge will stand this time. Built on true foundation."

But while hope flourished, resistance grew in equal measure. Those who had profited from division began to recognize the threat Geshriel posed to their power. Councillor Septus, whose authority derived from maintaining separation, watched the growing work with calculating eyes. Magistra Theoria, whose academic reputation rested on theories about why reconnection was impossible, circulated scrolls questioning Geshriel's methods. Vendors who had exploited scarcity saw their profits dwindle as Geshriel established fair trade practices within the village.

Their whispers became rumors, rumors became accusations. They claimed Geshriel's foundation would catastrophically fail, that his methods violated natural laws, that he was misleading vulnerable people with false hope.

When these tactics failed to halt progress, more direct opposition emerged. Work materials disappeared overnight. Completed sections were found damaged in ways that couldn't be accidental. Workers reported being threatened if they continued supporting Geshriel's project.

Through it all, Geshriel remained undeterred. When tools vanished, he designed new ones. When materials disappeared, he found alternatives. When threats scattered some workers, others arrived to take their place.

"They cannot stop what they don't understand," he told his followers one evening when particularly severe sabotage had been discovered. "They attack the bridge because they cannot attack its true foundation."

"Aren't you afraid?" asked a young woman who had found purpose in the work after years of despair. "They grow more dangerous each day."

Geshriel's smile held both compassion and certainty. "Perfect love casts out fear. What they intend for destruction will become the very means of completion."

The first direct threat to Geshriel's life came two months into the project. Fidel discovered it—a dark symbol painted on Geshriel's simple dwelling, a mark everyone recognized as a death threat. When he rushed to warn Geshriel, he found him already aware and strangely untroubled.

"You need protection," Fidel insisted. "These people are serious. They'll kill you to stop the bridge."

"They will," Geshriel agreed calmly. "It has always been the plan. What they think will stop the plan will actually complete the plan."

"What plan includes your murder?" Fidel demanded, shaken by his friend's acceptance.

Geshriel placed a hand on his shoulder. "The plan that has existed since before the bridge fell." His eyes held depths Fidel couldn't fathom. "The bridge, Fidel, can only be completed when the builder becomes the cornerstone."

The words sent a chill through Fidel's body. "You're speaking of sacrifice."

"The ultimate one," Geshriel confirmed. "Freely given, not taken."

"There must be another way," Fidel protested.

Geshriel's expression held infinite gentleness. "If there were, don't you think I would have taken it?"

That night, Fidel's hands trembled so violently the lantern scattered wild, fractured pulses across the dark—no pattern, just pain.

He tried to steady himself and signaled:

"Teacher speaks of ultimate sacrifice. Bridge completed through his death."

Geshriel's words still echoed in his mind. A bridge born through loss. A path that demanded more than stone. More than effort. It demanded him.

Across the river, her light returned with quiet clarity:

"Trust the teacher's wisdom. Path of love requires sacrifice."

Fidel stared at the signal, breath caught in his throat. After seven years of nightly communication, he could read the certainty in her responses. She wasn't confused. She wasn't shaken. She saw the same truth...and accepted it.

He raised the lantern once more—slowly—and traced their familiar signal:

"Hope still possible despite cost ahead?"

Her reply came quickly:

"Hope possible *because* cost ahead. Light conquers darkness. Love will be the foundation we stand on together."

And somehow, it was enough.

"It's not fair," he whispered into the darkness. "It's not right." Yet as the hours passed, something slowly unfolded within him—a recognition that the deepest truths often transcended simple notions of fairness.

By dawn, though still troubled, Fidel had reached a different understanding. Geshriel's sacrifice was somehow about both justice and love—the ultimate expression of what he had been teaching all along.

"I'm beginning to see," Fidel admitted, watching the sunrise, "that love is both gentler and fiercer than I ever imagined."

The next day, as the physical bridge took shape, rising now visibly above the water, Geshriel began preparing his closest followers for what would come. He taught them that entire day.

The structure, itself, was remarkable—unlike previous attempts focused on grand design, this bridge possessed a humble beauty born of function over form. Every element served a purpose. Nothing existed for mere show.

But at its center, spanning the deepest part of the river, a gap remained.

"This section cannot be built with ordinary materials," Geshriel explained, showing them drawings of the complete design. "It requires a special keystone." His eyes twinkled with an understanding that only he possessed.

"What does that mean?" several asked.

Instead of answering directly, Geshriel told them to meet him at the shore after sunset. They gathered as twilight painted the eastern sky golden while darkness claimed the west.

"The bridge stands half-complete," he said, gesturing to the structure extending from their shore. "But look across the river."

From the western shore, another half-bridge stretched toward them—similar in design, equally well-constructed. In the fading light, they could make out figures moving on its surface.

Gasps of surprise rippled through the group. "How is this possible?" someone asked. "Who leads them?"

Geshriel smiled. "The same spirit works on both shores, preparing for reunion."

For weeks now, their nightly communications had included daily progress reports from both sides. Verita had shared how the western community, inspired by Geshriel's teachings transmitted through Fidel's signals, had begun their own bridge using the same love-based foundation. Each night brought updates:

"Foundation complete on our side." "First supports raised today." "Gap narrowing between our bridges."

Fidel stared across the water, hope surging within him.

"The gap between the two halves," Geshriel continued, "can only be bridged by sacrifice. One life freely given creates the connection that ten thousand stones could never sustain."

The group fell silent, the implications of his words sinking in.

"You," a woman whispered finally. "You're speaking of yourself."

Geshriel nodded, his ordinary face illuminated with extraordinary purpose. "I came for this. To build a bridge that cannot fall, because its cornerstone is built by sacrificial love."

That night, Fidel's signals came quickly—his hands full of urgency.

"Can see other bridge reaching toward us. Gap narrowing to final span," he signaled.

Across the river, Verita's light responded with measured excitement:

"Almost time for reunion. Seven years of waiting nearly ended."

Fidel smiled faintly. After seven years of patient signaling, the end was in sight.

"Teacher speaks of ultimate sacrifice. Builder must become keystone for completion."

His hand paused. How could he explain the weight of what Geshriel meant to do?

"Sacrifice required for bridge success? True cost of love?" he sent.

Verita's reply came slowly, steadily:

"Trust teacher's plan completely. Story reaching proper ending."

Fidel lowered the lantern, the weight of her words settling deep in his chest. After seven years, this was it. The culmination of everything they'd endured.

The following dawn, Geshriel gathered his closest followers at the bridge's edge. The structure now extended impressively from both shores, the gap between reduced to perhaps thirty feet or less. With traditional methods, spanning this final section would be straightforward.

But Geshriel had never followed traditional methods.

"Today we prepare for completion," he announced. "The opposition will make its final move soon. They do not want the bridge to be finished—too much of their power depends on division."

"We'll protect you," several insisted. "They'll have to come through us first."

Geshriel shook his head, smiling with deep affection. "That is not the way. When they come for me, and they will, you must not fight. What appears as defeat will become victory. What seems like ending will become beginning."

"How can we let them take you?" Fidel demanded, unwilling to accept this path.

Geshriel placed both hands on Fidel's shoulders, his gaze penetrating to the soul. "Because only through my sacrifice can you be reunited with Verita. Only through my death can the broken bridge be made whole. Your faithful love, sustained across great distance, teaches what I came to demonstrate—that true love transcends every barrier, even death itself."

Geshriel turned to address them all. "Three days," he said. "In three days, the bridge will be complete. Those who have been separated will be reunited. What has been divided, love will restore."

He led them out onto the bridge, to the very edge where the gap began. Across the distance, figures had gathered on the opposite structure—pilgrims from the western shore preparing for the same culmination.

Fidel strained his eyes, searching for any glimpse of Verita among them on the western shore. Was she there, looking for him with equal longing? After seven years of darkness between them, was their reunion finally at hand? There were too many gathered, he could not find Verita.

Geshriel stood at the very edge, arms outstretched as if measuring the remaining gap with his body. For a moment—just a moment—his appearance seemed to shimmer, ordinary features briefly transfigured into something glorious.

"The cornerstone is ready," he said. "Now we wait for those who oppose unity to play their part. They believe they will destroy the bridge forever. Instead, they will complete what they most fear."

As they returned to shore, Fidel noticed men watching from shadows—Councilor Septus and his enforcers, Magistra Theoria with her academic followers, merchants whose wealth depended on continued separation. Their eyes tracked Geshriel's movements with cold calculation.

"They're definitely planning something," Fidel whispered.

"Yes," Geshriel agreed calmly. "And so am I."

That night, Fidel went to the signaling point on the shore, lantern in hand. Across the river, Verita's light appeared immediately—steady, urgent, expectant.

He raised his lantern and signaled:

"Three days until completion. Teacher prepares for ultimate sacrifice."

Geshriel had spoken with certainty. The work would be completed—through him. Fidel didn't fully understand. But he believed.

Her response came with calm conviction:

"Understanding grows of final mystery. Trust completely his plan."

"Will we truly stand together again after seven years?" he asked.

Her reply followed quickly:

"When sacrifice completes bridge work. Soon very soon."

Fidel exhaled, his hands trembling. After seven years of patient hope, she spoke with certainty, not mere wishful thinking.

He sent one final signal:

"Love endures all separation. Always faithful to you alone."

Across the river, her light answered in return:

"Same devotion here. Seven years of waiting nearly finished."

*Until the stars burn out,* he thought, watching her light dim for the night.

He lowered the lantern, river mist clinging to his skin like cold fingers. When he turned, Geshriel was there—watching him with infinite understanding.

"She waits faithfully," Geshriel smiled. "As do you."

"Seven years," Fidel confirmed, each word heavy with accumulated longing. "Each night choosing hope over the easier darkness."

Geshriel nodded, his eyes reflecting starlight. "Love counts every moment of separation. But soon, very soon, you will hold her again."

"Because of you," Fidel whispered, his throat closing around the words as understanding crushed down on him. "Because you will somehow become the bridge itself."

"Yes, the very cornerstone. I told you from the beginning—this bridge can only be built by sacrifice."

He turned to gaze across the river, his expression reflecting both anticipation and acceptance of what was to come.

"Watch for me on the third day," he said softly. "When darkness seems complete and hope seems lost, remember that death is not the final word. The bridge will stand. Love will prevail. Division will end."

As night deepened around them, the scent of wet stone and desperate hope heavy in the air, the churning river below raged as violently as ever, its chaotic waters reflecting no light, only churning darkness. For seven years the river had been a torrent of destruction, its surface too turbulent for any reflection, too dangerous for any crossing. In that moment, Fidel understood that Geshriel had been gradually preparing them for this culmination from the day he arrived—teaching them through quiet service and profound wisdom that the greatest bridges are built not of wood and stone, but of sacrifice freely given.

The true foundation was laid. The final cornerstone awaited placement.

## CHAPTER FOURTEEN

# The Keystone of Love

## GESHRIEL'S ACCOMPLISHMENT

The morning air hung heavy with anticipation as Fidel made his way to the bridge construction site. Long months of work under Geshriel's guidance had transformed not just the physical landscape but also the fabric of the community. The underwater foundation, invisible yet unshakable, now supported a structure extending halfway across the river. From the opposite shore, a mirror image stretched toward them, the gap between narrowing with each passing day.

But it was the gap within the village itself that had most remarkably closed. Fidel witnessed this transformation firsthand as he walked through the village that morning. Near the market square, he paused to watch two men working together to repair a damaged cart wheel—men he remembered as bitter rivals just months before. One held the wheel steady while the other fitted new spokes, their conversation easy and collaborative.

"Hand me that smaller hammer," the first man requested.

"The one your grandfather made?" the second replied, passing the tool with a smile. "My father always said it was the finest in the village."

"Your father had good eyes for craftsmanship," came the warm response.

Fidel marveled at the exchange. These same two men had once refused to speak to each other, their families divided by a property dispute that had festered for years.

Where once faction fought faction, neighbors now shared meals. Where suspicion once poisoned every interaction, trust now flourished like the newly revived gardens. Geshriel had built bridges between hearts before a single stone was laid in the river.

"Today we enter the final phase," Geshriel announced to the gathered workers, his ordinary appearance belying the extraordinary authority in his voice. "The bridge stands ready for completion."

Fidel, now twenty-nine and bearing the weight of years of separation, noticed how Geshriel's gaze lingered on the center gap—the space where the eastern and western segments would finally meet. According to all engineering principles, this connection should be straightforward. Yet Geshriel had spoken repeatedly of a keystone that would be unlike any other.

"Will we finish today?" asked an eager young worker, hope brightening his face—an expression once rare in this village broken by years of failed attempts.

Geshriel smiled gently. "The completion comes precisely when it must. Not before." His eyes swept across the assembled villagers. "Those who oppose unity have already set their plans in motion. They move against us even now."

A murmur passed through the crowd. Everyone knew of the growing resistance—Councillor Septus and his border enforcement, Magistra Theoria with her academic followers, the merchants whose wealth depended on continued separation. Their whispered threats had become increasingly open in recent days.

"Let them try to stop us," declared a burly stonemason, raising a calloused fist. "We'll defend you—and the bridge."

Geshriel shook his head, his expression serene yet somehow sorrowful. "That is not the way. When they come, and they will come, you must not fight. What appears as defeat will become victory."

Fidel studied his friend's face, troubled by the certainty with which Geshriel spoke of coming violence. Years of watching hope die repeatedly had taught him to recognize the signs. "There must be another way," he insisted, stepping closer.

Geshriel placed a hand on Fidel's shoulder, his touch conveying both affection and resolve. "The bridge can only be completed through sacrifice freely given. It was planned this way, from the foundation of the world."

***

As the workers dispersed to their tasks, Fidel remained at Geshriel's side, watching as he traced the bridge's arc with his eyes, seeming to measure distances only he could fully perceive. Fidel noticed Demas lingering at the edge of the group, his face troubled. The young man had grown increasingly quiet during Geshriel's recent teachings about becoming the keystone, often slipping away when the conversations turned to sacrifice. Now he stood apart, his eyes shifting between Geshriel and the village center where opposition leaders had been gathering.

"You've known this from the beginning, haven't you?" Fidel asked quietly, his voice carrying the weariness of a man who had endured repeated disappointment. "Since the day you arrived, you've been preparing for this moment."

Geshriel nodded, his ordinary features momentarily illuminated with extraordinary purpose. "From before the bridge fell, this has been the plan. The keystone was ready before the foundation was laid."

Throughout the day, tension mounted. Fidel saw it clearly when one of Septus' enforcers approached a young bridge worker who was mixing mortar.

"You there," the enforcer barked, pointing at the worker's bucket. "What's in that mixture?"

The worker looked up nervously. "Just... mortar, sir. Sand, lime, water."

The enforcer dipped his finger into the mixture, then sniffed it suspiciously. "Looks contaminated to me. Could weaken the structure." He turned to his companion. "Make a note—substandard materials."

The young worker's face reddened with indignation, but he said nothing, returning to his work with clenched jaw.

Nearby, one of Magistra Theoria's scribes pointed at the spots where Geshriel's blood from hours of work had stained the bridge stones months earlier. "See these discolorations?" she announced loudly to her fellow scholars. "Clear evidence of structural weakness. This bridge is fundamentally flawed."

Septus' enforcers circled the site, making notes and exchanging signals. Magistra Theoria's scribes documented the bridge, searching for flaws to exploit, pointing out the colored stains on the bridge and calling them "weaknesses." Merchants held furtive meetings, scowling when workers passed.

By sunset, Geshriel led his closest followers onto the bridge itself, walking to the very edge where the gap began. Fidel gazed across the remaining distance, perhaps twenty feet of rushing water separating the two sides. On the opposite structure, figures had gathered, similarly positioned at their edge. Fidel searched intently for Verita; he thought he spotted her in the crowd—twenty-six now, a woman grown, no longer the nineteen-year-old girl he had known before their long separation had aged them both.

"Tomorrow," Geshriel said, his voice carried easily across the water, "the division ends. What years of separation have stolen will be restored in a single moment."

As darkness fell, Fidel noticed a shadowy figure slipping away from their group, moving quickly toward the village center where Septus and the opposition leaders had established their headquarters. The betrayal had begun.

Geshriel placed a gentle hand on Fidel's shoulder. "Go," he said softly. "Signal to her one last time before they come. Tell her what tomorrow will bring."

Fidel nodded, understanding. He made his way back along the bridge to the eastern shore, then to his familiar signaling post at the riverbank.

***

That night, Fidel maintained his vigil at the riverbank, raising his lantern in the familiar signal to Verita. Her answering light appeared immediately, as if she'd been waiting with unusual urgency.

"Thought I saw you today among the gathered crowd," he signaled using their sophisticated code.

"Something momentous happens tomorrow. Geshriel speaks of ultimate sacrifice. Opposition forces gathering dangerous strength."

"Same developments here on western shore," came her response, each signal deliberate and clear.

"Not certain I saw you clearly, or just my heart desperately saw you. Our teacher says bridge completed through living keystone sacrifice."

"After so long separation, can hardly believe reunion finally possible," Fidel continued, his hands trembling slightly with the weight of accumulated emotion and hope deferred.

"Believe completely, Fidel," she urged through the complex signal patterns.

"Love proves stronger than death itself. Stronger than raging river."

"Until the stars burn out completely," he signaled, their traditional closing phrase that had sustained them through the darkness.

"Until the stars burn out completely," she replied with steady certainty. "And far beyond that promise."

***

A commotion erupted from the village center—angry voices, the glow of torches, the sound of many feet marching with purpose. Fidel quickly secured his lantern and hurried back toward the bridge, where he found Geshriel waiting calmly at the eastern entrance, watching the approaching mob with an expression of complete acceptance.

"They come," Geshriel said simply as Fidel reached his side. "The hour has arrived."

"We must hide you," Fidel insisted, reaching for his friend's arm. Years of watching saviors fall had taught him the signs of approaching catastrophe. "There's still time to—"

"This is precisely where I must be," Geshriel interrupted gently. "At the bridge's edge, ready to become what I have always been meant to be."

The evening shadows lengthened as the mob surged toward them, led by Councillor Septus, his face twisted with righteous indignation. Beside him marched Magistra Theoria, clutching scrolls that presumably documented Geshriel's "crimes." Behind them came the merchants, the self-appointed religious leaders, and enforcers armed with clubs and ropes—all those who had profited from division.

"There he is!" Septus shouted, pointing at Geshriel. "The deceiver who threatens our established order with his talk of unity!"

"The heretic who contradicts all accepted wisdom!" added Magistra Theoria.

"The revolutionary who would destroy our profitable separation!" cried a merchant who had grown wealthy from enforced scarcity.

Geshriel stood perfectly still, making no move to flee or defend himself as the mob surrounded him. His closest followers gathered protectively, but with a slight gesture, he signaled them to step aside.

"If you seek me," he said calmly, "then let these others go. This moment is between us."

To Fidel's shock, a figure emerged from behind Septus—Demas, one of their own circle who had worked alongside them for months. His face could not meet Geshriel's eyes but rather greeted him with a kiss on the cheek.

The betrayal cut deep. Geshriel, however, showed no surprise. As the enforcers moved to seize him, he addressed Demas directly: "You have played your part in completing the plan."

The mob bound Geshriel's hands and led him away, jeering and mocking as they went. Their torches cast wild shadows across the village square, creating a grotesque scene of shifting darkness and harsh light. Fidel and the other followers trailed behind, their hearts heavy with dread yet unable to abandon their teacher.

***

Throughout the night, they held a mockery of justice. First at Septus's chambers, where the councilor interrogated Geshriel for hours about his teachings and intentions. Then to Magistra Theoria's academy, where scholars ridiculed his simple wisdom and spat upon his bloodied face. Finally, before dawn, to the merchants' guild hall, where they stripped him of his garments and beat him with rods, each blow punctuated with accusations of undermining their profitable separation.

Through it all, Geshriel remained largely silent, answering only when necessary and with words that seemed to pierce his accusers to their core.

"What authority do you claim?" demanded Septus during one particularly vicious questioning.

"The authority of love," Geshriel replied simply. "Which neither seeks nor requires position."

"And what wisdom do you possess that contradicts our established knowledge?" Magistra Theoria sneered.

"The wisdom that sees division as illness, not health, as rebellion, not submission." Geshriel answered. "And separation as exposure, not protection."

As the first light of dawn touched the eastern horizon, they dragged Geshriel, now barely able to stand from the night's abuse, to the bridge's edge. A crowd had gathered, drawn by rumors of the night's events. Some wept openly at the sight of Geshriel's battered form, while others jeered, caught up in the frenzy of hatred fed by accumulated bitterness. Pulling him forward every step, they led him to the center point of the bridge.

As the village bell finished nine strikes, Septus gave the order: "Prepare him for execution."

Two thick wooden beams were brought forward and laid upon the ground near the bridge's edge. The enforcers positioned them to cross each other—one beam longer than the other, both hewn from the strongest timber.

They forced Geshriel down onto the beams. He went willingly. His tunic, already torn and bloodied from the night's brutality, was ripped away completely. Against the rough wood, they pressed his back, still raw from the whipping he had endured.

With methodical cruelty, they stretched his arms wide across the horizontal beam and drove iron spikes through his palms, anchoring him to the wood with terrible finality. Then they bound his feet to the vertical beam with coarse rope. The sound of metal piercing flesh, a wet, sickening thud, cut through the crowd's murmurs. Geshriel's breath caught, a sharp moan between clenched teeth. The wood beneath him darkened instantly, drinking in his blood with eager thirst. A scent like heated copper mingled with the river's damp mist, metallic and primal.

A cry went up from some of his followers at this ultimate brutality. Fidel's hands clenched into fists so tight his nails drew blood, every muscle screaming to rush forward, to tear Geshriel free from the wood. Years of helplessness in the face of tragedy had not prepared him for this moment of ultimate powerlessness. But Geshriel's earlier words echoed: "You must not fight." His knees gave way, his body collapsing under the weight of enforced helplessness. Geshriel's face contorted with agony, yet from his lips came no curse, no scream—only a soft exhalation that seemed to carry both pain and purpose.

"Lift him up," Septus commanded. "Let all see what becomes of those who challenge the established order."

Using ropes and pulleys, they hoisted the wooden beams with Geshriel fastened to them, raising him high above the crowd so that everyone on both shores could witness his suffering. The contraption was positioned at the very edge of the eastern bridge.

His arms stretched wide across the horizontal beam, as if reaching from one side toward the other in an embrace that couldn't quite be completed. Blood dripped from his wounds into the churning waters below, each crimson drop creating tiny circles that expanded outward before being swept away by the current.

Fidel watched in horror, every fiber of his being crying out against this injustice. Then Geshriel's eyes found his across the distance; not filled with despair but with such profound love that Fidel felt embraced despite the terrible gap between them.

Time suspended itself, the way it had in Harmonia's studio when golden light had painted Verita's face years ago. But this was different—deeper. In Geshriel's gaze, Fidel saw not the breathless wonder of a lover, but something infinitely larger: the way he loved Verita, magnified beyond measure, extended to encompass not just him but every soul watching. Love without limit, and without end. Love that would die to connect what had been broken.

As Geshriel hung suspended between heaven and earth, between the Creator and the creation, something remarkable became visible to those who watched. In his suffering, he was fulfilling what all the previous builders had sought but never achieved.

Here was Regulus's perfect standard made flesh—not demanding perfection from others, but becoming perfect sacrifice himself. His flawless love showed what true law was meant to accomplish: not accusation and condemnation, but redemption and connection.

Here was Sophia's ultimate wisdom revealed—not in scrolls or theories, but in the living demonstration that love's sacrifice bridges what knowledge alone cannot span. All the understanding they had sought was embodied in this moment of self-giving.

Here was Ritus's perfect ritual—not empty ceremony, but the living sacrifice that gave meaning to all symbols. Every ancient practice had pointed to this moment when the sacrifice would be real, personal, and transformative.

Here was Altruia's complete service—not the exhausting labor that turns inward, but the ultimate act of serving others by laying down one's life. This was service that would never end because it was grounded in infinite love.

Here was Optimus's true belief made manifest—not the positive thinking that denied reality, but the faith that faced the worst of reality and still chose love. This was hope that could never be disappointed because it was rooted in self-sacrifice rather than self-assertion.

Here was Metamorphia's real transformation—not the superficial changing of identity, but the profound metamorphosis brought about by forgiveness, hatred becoming love, defeat becoming victory, division becoming unity. The ultimate change that would affect not just one person, but restore connection between all who had been separated.

"It is necessary," Geshriel whispered, his voice somehow reaching Fidel alone despite the wind and the crowd's murmurs. "The bridge... must be... completed. For you... for all."

\*\*\*

The morning hours passed with unbearable slowness as Geshriel suffered. Some mocked him, challenging him to save himself if he truly had the power to build bridges. Others watched in silent horror, unable to intervene yet unwilling to leave. Fidel remained closest, his eyes rarely leaving his teacher's face, drawing on seven years of patient waiting to sustain him through this ultimate test.

From his suspended position, Geshriel spoke words of love even to those who tormented him. When a posted guard offered him bitter wine to mock his thirst, Geshriel looked at the man with such compassion that the soldier stepped back in confusion. "You do not know what you do," Geshriel said gently. "But you are forgiven."

To the merchants who had orchestrated his death to protect their profits, he said, "Your greed has blinded you to the treasure you could have shared. But love can open even the most closed heart."

To Magistra Theoria, who continued to shout scholarly objections to his teachings, he replied, "True wisdom is not found in books alone, but in the willingness to love without return."

As the sun climbed toward its zenith, something extraordinary began to happen. Just as the village bell tolled the twelfth hour of day, the sky, which had been clear moments before, suddenly darkened. Clouds rolled in with unnatural speed, blotting out the sun entirely. It was midnight at midday. The temperature dropped sharply, a cold wind whipping around the bridge.

"What sorcery is this?" someone cried, pointing at the unnaturally darkened sky.

Geshriel's breathing grew labored, each exhale sending ripples of pain across his tortured frame. Yet from his lips came not curses but unexpected words of blessing: "Creator, forgive them... they act from fear and misunderstanding..."

The first rumble came as a distant vibration, felt through the soles of their feet before it registered in their ears. The crowd grew uneasy, memories of the original catastrophic earthquake suddenly fresh in every mind.

"This is your doing!" Septus accused, pointing at Geshriel. "You bring destruction as the others did!"

Geshriel raised his head with tremendous effort, his voice somehow carrying above the growing wind. "Not destruction... completion."

A second, stronger tremor shook the bridge. Unlike the earthquake that had destroyed the original span, this vibration seemed to resonate with the structure, causing it to hum rather than crack. The stones beneath their feet grew warm.

Lightning cracked across the sky, illuminating the scene in harsh relief. In that brilliant flash, witnesses on both shores could clearly see each other across the gap. Fidel glimpsed a female figure on the western edge—Verita, her face turned toward the unfolding tragedy, her hand outstretched as if trying to reach across the divide that had separated them for so long.

The third tremor brought thunder that shook the air itself. The bridge vibrated with increasing intensity, yet instead of showing signs of stress, the structure seemed to be strengthening, the stones fitting more tightly together, the mortar hardening to unprecedented density.

Geshriel's suffering reached its crescendo. His body convulsed, his outstretched arms trembling with the weight they bore. Rain began to fall—first as gentle drops, then as a deluge that washed his blood across the bridge's surface. Where the diluted blood touched, the stone transformed, taking on a luminous quality.

"I'm...thirsty." Geshriel gasped. Fidel remembered Geshriel offering him "water that would not run dry", and felt the irony of it. It was as if Geshriel thirsted so Fidel's thirst of reunion could be quenched.

Another lightning flash, closer now, followed immediately by deafening thunder. The earth beneath the river itself seemed to convulse, the water churning with unprecedented force.

Geshriel summoned his remaining strength, lifting his head one final time. "I love you...I forgive you," he declared, his voice suddenly strong and clear despite his failing body. And with one more effort, he said with a loud voice, what sounded more like victory than defeat.

"All is complete."

With these words, he slowly bowed his head, as if in worship, and breathed his last.

As life left him, a heavy silence fell over both shores. Then something impossible began to happen.

At the moment of Geshriel's death, those watching the bridge gasped in amazement. The stains that had marred the structure—the sickly green of greed, the inky black of deception, the blue of fear—began to dissolve as if washed away by an invisible tide. Where corruption had marked the stone, now gleamed surfaces pure and clean. The shame that had been evidenced in those discolorations vanished completely, leaving behind only the luminous foundation of love.

The wooden beams, with Geshriel's lifeless form attached, began to fall forward—not tumbling chaotically, but moving with deliberate, supernatural purpose. The vertical beam that had stood upright now rotated to become horizontal as the entire structure tilted across the gap. The weight and momentum carried it perfectly across the twenty-foot divide until the far end of what had been the vertical beam locked precisely into prepared grooves on the western bridge's edge, as if the construction had been designed exactly for this moment.

The beam, now supported at both ends, spanned the gap completely. Geshriel's body lay stretched across the divide, his arms still extended along the crossbeam, his form now bridging east and west in literal fact.

Fidel watched in amazement as the impossible unfolded before them. Geshriel's sacrifice had not only been spiritual—it had become the very physical connection they had sought through six failed attempts over seven years of struggle.

But the transformation was not complete. As witnesses on both sides stared in awe, Geshriel's broken body began to change. The blood that had flowed freely from his wounds now coursed with luminous purpose, tracing patterns of light along the wooden beams. His flesh, blood, and bone began to blur, dissolving into the wood that held him, which in turn began to transform into something neither timber nor stone but somehow both.

Septus, who had ordered this execution with such righteous certainty, fell to his knees, his face transformed by dawning horror and recognition. "What have we done?" he whispered, then louder: "What have I done? Truly this Man was Love Incarnate!"

The transformation accelerated. Where Geshriel's heart had been, a brilliant light sent waves of radiance along the spanning structure. His form was becoming one with the bridge itself, his sacrifice literally becoming the connection that would never fail.

Workers and opposition alike stood transfixed as Geshriel's body merged completely with the wooden beams, which then transformed into a substance that matched the rest of the bridge perfectly. Where wood had been, now stood a span of luminous stone.

The light from the center grew blindingly bright, forcing many to shield their eyes. When they could look again, the gap was gone. Where Geshriel had died stretched across the divide, a perfect keystone now connected the two halves of the bridge. The structure was complete, seamless, radiant with an inner light.

Below them, the churning waters that had raged with fury for seven years suddenly stilled. The river, as if repenting of its wrath, turned from violence to peace. Where once the current had torn at everything it touched with destructive force, now the water flowed freely and smoothly, reflecting the bridge's luminous glow like liquid starlight. Even nature itself had been transformed by Geshriel's sacrifice.

A hush fell over both shores. Rain continued to fall, but gently now, cleansing the bridge and washing away the tools of execution. The wooden beams were gone, yet their form remained visible in the pattern of the keystone—arms outstretched from a central point, embracing both east and west in perfect unity.

Fidel approached the connection point with trembling steps, his twenty-nine-year-old body carrying the weight of waiting. The bridge felt different beneath his feet—like he was standing on the foundation of love itself. When he reached the center, he knelt, placing his hand on the keystone. Warmth radiated from it, along with a sense of presence so familiar it brought tears to his eyes.

"Geshriel," he whispered. "You are the bridge."

From the western side, a figure moved toward him—walking carefully toward the newly completed span. Though he had not seen her face in so long, and though she was at quite a distance, Fidel would have recognized her anywhere.

The bridge that Geshriel had promised, the living bridge built through ultimate sacrifice, stood complete. The impossible had become possible. Love Incarnate had spanned what no human effort could bridge after years of failed attempts.

Division had ended. Unity had begun. And at the center of it all was the reminder that the greatest bridges are built not of stone and wood, but of love strong enough to lay itself down for others.

The Broken Bridge was now made whole by the Keystone of Love.

# CHAPTER FIFTEEN

# The Reunion

## WHAT LOVE RESTORED

The keystone rested cool and still beneath Fidel's palm—unmoving, unchanging, the stone placed with finality. He remained kneeling at the center of the bridge, hollowed by what he had just witnessed. Geshriel had given everything, embraced death fully, without resistance. His sacrifice had not preserved him—it had ended him. And yet, in that ending, the bridge now stood complete, a new beginning for all. The power was not in Geshriel surviving, but in his death making a way for others to cross.

From the western shore, a figure approached—walking with deliberate steps toward the newly completed span. Though distance still blurred her features, Fidel would have recognized that silhouette anywhere. He rose slowly to his feet, his body suddenly lighter than it had been in years.

"Verita," he whispered, his voice catching on her name.

She moved toward him with measured steps at first, as if testing the solidity of this miracle beneath her feet. Fidel found himself mirroring her caution, taking one tentative step, then another. The bridge held firm—unlike all previous attempts, this structure felt not just solid but responsive to their weight, almost cradling their footfalls.

Their pace quickened simultaneously, as if orchestrated by a silent conductor. Recognition bloomed fully on Verita's face. He could see it clearly now, her eyes widening, her lips forming his name though he was still too far to hear it. His own heart thundered in his chest, pushing him forward, faster now.

What began as careful steps transformed into an urgent walk, then a jog, and finally a desperate sprint. They ran toward each other across Geshriel's bridge, seven years of separation collapsing with each footfall.

They collided at last in an embrace so fierce it nearly toppled them both. Fidel's arms encircled her completely, lifting her off her feet as momentum spun them in a circle. Her arms locked around his neck with equal intensity, her face buried in his neck.

No words came—none were needed. Just as they had signaled across the darkness, their reunion began with nothing but the profound eloquence of touch. Fidel held her exactly as he had promised, saying nothing, just feeling their hearts beating against each other, syncopating gradually until they seemed to pulse as one.

Tears flowed freely between them, mingling on their cheeks. Sobs gave way to breathless laughter, which turned again to weeping, the emotions cycling through them too complex for any single expression. Around them, other reunions were beginning to unfold as brave souls from both shores ventured across the miraculous span.

"You're real," Verita finally whispered against his neck, her first words to him in over seven years. "You're really here."

Fidel drew back just enough to see her face—the face he had dreamed of every night, the features he had described to himself each morning to ensure he would never forget a detail. She was thinner than before, with new lines of sorrow and resilience etched around her eyes. Her chestnut hair was longer now, woven with braids that spoke of patient hours spent alone. But her eyes—those eyes that had always reflected truth, remained unchanged in their essential nature.

"I can't believe I'm actually seeing you," he choked out the words through tears, his hands framing her face as if to convince himself she was real. "You're more beautiful than I remembered."

"I promised," he said simply, his voice raw. "Until the stars burned out. And beyond."

She smiled then, the expression he had longed for through endless nights of lantern signals. "And I kept watch at the river's edge. Every night, waiting for your light." Her fingers traced the line of his jaw.

Their lips met in a kiss that held seven years of separation, longing, and faithful love. When they finally parted, both were breathless.

Fidel reached into his pocket and withdrew the small wooden bird she had carved for him—worn smooth by years of anxious handling, its original details faded, but its essence intact, just as their love had endured despite separation.

"It never left me," he told her, placing it in her palm. "Every night I held it while I signaled to you."

Verita's fingers closed around the carving. With her other hand, she reached for something secured beneath her collar; a silver chain from which hung a pendant that mirrored the wooden bird, one she had carved herself from river stone during their separation.

"I made this to match yours," she explained. "I would hold it each night while signaling to you, imagining someday placing it in your hands." She pressed it into his palm, their fingers intertwining. "Now I never want to let go."

Other reunited couples moved around them, embracing, weeping, exclaiming in joy and disbelief. Young people found parents they barely remembered. Siblings who had grown into strangers rediscovered their connection.

Near the bridge's center, Garus the stonemason stood with shaking hands, no longer from drink but from overwhelming emotion. Three figures approached from the western shore—a woman with graying hair and two young women, the younger one now tall and graceful, no longer the child he'd lost seven years ago.

"Elara?" he whispered, hardly daring to believe.

His wife's face crumpled with joy and relief. "Garus. We never stopped hoping you'd find your way back to us."

For a moment, no one moved, the weight of seven years hanging between them. Then his older daughter broke first, rushing into his arms. "Papa, I thought you were dead for seven years. We all did."

Garus held her fiercely, his voice breaking. "I was dead, in every way that mattered. But I'm alive now because I get to see you again." He looked over her shoulder at his younger daughter, who hung back uncertainly. "Roselyn?"

She stepped forward slowly, studying his face. "You look... different. Older. But your eyes..." She reached up tentatively to touch his cheek. "I remember your eyes", she said with tears flowing down her cheeks.

"Every freckle," he marveled, his voice thick with wonder as he drew her into the embrace. "I can see every freckle again. You're so tall, so beautiful. Both of you." He looked at Elara, his wife, extending one arm to include her. "Forgive me. I lost myself completely. But Geshriel...he showed me how to find my way home."

The four of them stood together on the bridge that sacrifice had built, a family made whole again.

Even as these scenes unfolded all along the bridge, Fidel and Verita remained in their own sacred space, drinking in each other's presence.

"He told me this would happen," Fidel said, his gaze shifting briefly to the cornerstone that had once been Geshriel. "He said the bridge would stand. That love would prevail."

Verita nodded, tears welling again. "The transformation of the cornerstone, connecting what division had separated."

## The Wedding Ceremony

On the second day since Geshriel's sacrifice, villagers from both shores gathered at the bridge's center for a wedding ceremony that couldn't wait.

Among the gathered crowd, Harmonia moved with purposeful energy, her arms full of the same yellow wildflowers that would soon adorn Verita's hair. Seven years ago, she had spent weeks planning every detail of this couple's wedding, only to watch the earthquake destroy everything in a single, devastating moment. The guilt had haunted her—all those careful preparations reduced to rubble. But today, as she wove the delicate blooms into garlands and arranged them around the sacred keystone, tears of joy streamed down her face. "This time," she whispered to herself, securing the final arrangement, "this time nothing will stop their happiness." The bridge itself seemed to respond to her touch, the flowers taking root in the living stone as if blessing her faithful service.

Elder Pax from Eastlight and Elder Benedict from Westshore stood ready to officiate, their voices carrying across the water as they spoke of love's persistence through trial.

"Today, we complete what was interrupted," said Elder Pax, who had once muttered "Hope deferred makes the heart sick" in his despair, but now stood radiant with joy. "Not merely resuming where we left off, but beginning anew with deeper understanding."

Fidel stood near the keystone, dressed in ceremonial garments adorned with symbols of unity. Geshriel's followers had arranged flowers in a circle around the cornerstone.

When Verita appeared at the western end of the bridge, escorted by Uncle Aldric in his ceremonial night watchman's cloak, a hush fell over the gathered community. Verita looked stunningly radiant, a bride who had made herself ready. The kind old man walked with dignified pride, his arm linked with the woman he had raised as his own daughter.

Verita wore a simple gown of ivory linen, her chestnut hair adorned with yellow wildflowers that Harmonia had woven in just moments before—the same blooms she had planned to use seven years ago, finally fulfilling their destined purpose. In her hands,

Verita carried not a bouquet of flowers, but a single lantern, the same one she had raised night after night to connect with Fidel across the river.

As she walked toward him, Fidel was struck by the symmetry of this moment—how it both echoed and transformed the memory of their interrupted wedding seven years earlier. Then, they had taken their connection for granted, assuming the bridge would always be there. Now, having endured seven years apart, they understood the precious fragility and stubborn persistence of love.

When they reached Fidel, Uncle Aldric gently took Verita's lantern and placed it beside Fidel's on the keystone. Then, with tears brightening his crinkly eyes, he placed his niece's hand in Fidel's. "She's been waiting for this moment as faithfully as you have," he whispered, his voice thick with emotion. "I raised her to know the value of keeping promises." He squeezed both their hands. "Take care of each other." Then he stepped back, his duty as surrogate father lovingly complete.

Fidel took Verita's hands in his, the familiar contours of her fingers filling spaces that had remained empty for too long.

"I, Fidel, take you, Verita," he began, his voice trembling with emotion, "my beloved who waited in faithfulness. You are the light that guided me through every dark night, the hope that sustained me through every failed attempt to reach you. I promise to love you not just with the desperate longing that carried me through our separation, but with the deep, sacrificial love that Geshriel showed us—love that seeks your good above my own desires. You are my heart's home, and I will never take our love for granted again."

Tears streamed down Verita's face, but her voice remained steady—true to her name. "I, Verita, take you, Fidel, the man whose signals were my lifeline when all seemed lost. Your light never wavered, your love never faltered. I learned to love you not just as the boy I fell for, but as the man you became through suffering—patient, faithful, strong. I promise to be your truth-speaker, your companion, your joy. What Geshriel's sacrifice made possible, I vow to honor with every breath. You waited for me, believed in us, never gave up—now let me spend my lifetime showing you that your faithfulness was not in vain."

As the ceremony reached its culmination, Fidel reached into his pocket and withdrew the small wooden box that had survived the original collapse. The bent hinges caught the bridge's gentle radiance as he opened it to reveal the amber pendant, the Eternus bloom still glowing white and perfect within.

"I meant to give this to you on our wedding day seven years ago," he said softly, his voice carrying across the gathered community. "It survived the earthquake, the destruction, and all the years between. Like our love."

Verita's eyes filled with tears as he placed the pendant around her neck. "The bloom that never fades," she whispered, touching the amber gently. "From the western shore where I waited for you."

The pendant settled against her heart, completing a promise begun long ago and preserved through the darkest of separations.

They kissed then, deeply and passionately, as the gathered community erupted in joyous celebration.

"What Geshriel joined together," Elder Pax declared, "let nothing divide."

## The Transformation

The hours that followed were filled with both wonder and necessary planning. Both communities, separated for so long, now faced the immediate joy of reunion alongside the complexity of reintegration. The bridge provided the physical connection, but profound changes were already visible in those who stepped upon it.

Most remarkable were the changes in those who had opposed Geshriel. Councillor Septus stood apart from the celebrations, his proud bearing visibly shaken. Unlike the joy surrounding him, his face was etched with the beginnings of a terrible recognition—the first glimpse of what he had done.

"I might as well have driven in the nails myself," he said quietly to those who approached him, his voice shaky. His hands, the same that had ordered Geshriel's execution, trembled as he spoke. "Every decision I made to preserve our separation, every family I kept divided—it all led to his death."

He paused, watching a family embrace nearby. "I was so certain that maintaining our separation was necessary—that it protected us. I couldn't see..." His words trailed off. The weight of understanding was too fresh, too raw for easy confession.

"Geshriel spoke forgiveness with his dying breath," he continued, his voice breaking. "But I don't know how to receive it yet. I don't know how to undo what I've done." The admission hung heavy in the air—the desperate uncertainty of someone just beginning to see the magnitude of their failures. He turned to help a limping old man navigate a difficult section of the bridge.

Magistra Theoria stood among her former students, but for the first time in years, she had no lectures to give. The scholar who had built her reputation on theories of inevitable division now found herself speechless, her certainties crumbling.

"My greatest failure," she began hesitantly, her usual academic authority replaced by something more fragile, "was believing that understanding was the same as wisdom. I dissected truth until it died in my hands, then charged others to view the lifeless remains."

She touched the keystone with uncertain fingers. "Geshriel showed me that truth isn't merely something to be analyzed, but someone to be known and loved. But I..." she paused, struggling. "I spent so many years teaching division that I don't know how to teach unity. I don't even know where to begin."

One of her former students stepped forward. "Perhaps," he said gently, "you could start by learning alongside us."

Theoria's eyes filled with tears. "I'm not sure I know how to do that anymore. But I have to try." Her academy would need to be completely rebuilt, her life's work reconsidered. The path ahead seemed impossibly difficult, but for the first time, she was willing to begin walking it.

Unlike Septus and Magistra Theoria, Demas never witnessed the completion of the bridge he had unwittingly helped create through betrayal. The morning after Geshriel's execution, they found his body hanging from a twisted tree on the eastern cliffs, his despair having driven him to take his own life. Among the transformed community, his absence stood as a sorrowful reminder that even the greatest forgiveness must be *received* to bring restoration.

## The Evening

As sunset approached, Fidel and Verita moved through the celebration, helping with preparations while barely able to separate from each other. They worked side by side, hands touching whenever possible, stealing glances and soft words.

"I keep thinking you'll disappear," Fidel murmured as they arranged flowers near the bridge's eastern approach. "That this is another dream."

"I'm here," Verita whispered back, squeezing his hand. "Real and never leaving your side again."

By sunset, the bridge had become their center. Plants sprouted from crevices where Geshriel's blood had touched, yielding flowers with healing properties. The keystone seemed to glow more brightly whenever acts of love took place upon it, as if reflecting the memory of Geshriel's sacrifice.

Most remarkably, those who stepped onto the living bridge reported unexpected healing—not just emotional but physical.

Fidel and Verita witnessed one such moment as they helped arrange the evening celebration. An elderly woman hobbled onto the bridge, leaning heavily on a walking stick, her face tight with years of chronic pain. She moved slowly toward a middle-aged man who stood uncertainly near the keystone.

"Mother?" the man called out hesitantly.

The elderly woman's eyes filled with tears. "My son. Oh my son." Her voice was barely a whisper.

"I'm sorry," he said, stepping closer. "I'm so sorry I left in anger. I've regretted it for seven years."

As they embraced, something remarkable happened. The woman's walking stick clattered to the stone as her arms wrapped around her son. She stood straight for the first time in years, the lines of pain smoothing from her face.

"My back," she gasped, pulling away to look at him in wonder. "The pain...it's gone." She took several steps without assistance, her eyes bright with amazement. "Seven years of constant aching, and now..."

Fidel and Verita exchanged awestruck glances.

A man's chronic pain from an old injury vanished when he reconnected with his estranged brother. A woman's trembling hands grew steady as she embraced the neighbor she had blamed for her son's death. It seemed the bridge didn't merely connect the physical shores—it mended broken connections of all kinds.

As the wedding festivities wound down and most families began returning to their homes, Fidel took Verita's hand with unmistakable purpose.

"I need to be alone with you," Fidel whispered, seven years of separation making his desire urgent. "I need to hold you without anyone watching, to tell you everything I couldn't say in signals."

Verita's eyes sparkled with the same longing. "I've dreamed of that too. Of really being yours, completely."

They began walking purposefully toward the western shore, toward the small dwelling that would be theirs for this first night together as husband and wife. As they walked,

Fidel's pace quickened with each step, his eagerness infectious, until he was nearly pulling Verita behind him, both of them laughing. Fidel was on a mission.

"Slow down!" Verita gasped between giggles, "or you'll have us both tumbling into the river!"

"I can't help it," Fidel laughed, "I've waited seven years for this moment—I'm not waiting another second longer than necessary!"

## The Promise of Tomorrow

As they reached the western end of the bridge, they paused briefly to look back at the structure that had made their reunion possible, their hearts awash with gratitude to Geshriel.

"He said something to me that night," Fidel recalled, his voice quiet with reverence. "Just before they took him. He said, 'Watch for me on the third day. When darkness seems complete and hope seems lost, remember that death is not the final word.'"

Verita nodded, remembering how Geshriel had taught about seeds dying to produce new life. "Tomorrow is the third day," she whispered.

"I feel drawn to come here at dawn," Fidel said. "What if...what if he meant it literally?"

But as they stood at the threshold of Verita's dwelling, the promise of tomorrow seemed distant compared to the reality of tonight.

"Seven years," Fidel murmured as they finally reached the door. "Seven years I've dreamed of holding you like this. Of showing you the love I couldn't convey through signaling."

"Then stop talking," Verita whispered, her eyes bright with love and anticipation, "and start showing me."

As the door closed behind them, the bridge glowed softly in the starlight, a testament to love that had overcome every barrier, ready to witness whatever the third day might bring.

# CHAPTER SIXTEEN

# Author's Note

Thank you for reading!

Ephesians 2:16 says, *"...reconciling both of them to God in one body through the cross"*.

*The Broken Bridge* tells a story of division and healing through sacrificial love. It draws from the Christian narrative that has transformed my life—that sin separated humanity from God, breaking our relationships, and that Jesus Christ became the bridge to restore what was lost through His self-giving love.

The Christian story of the gospel is not an allegory, not a fable or myth; it is a historically accurate, well-documented truth. It was prophesied thousands of years before it happened. My hope is that you will want to know Geshriel, whose real name is Jesus Christ, the one who died for your sins and rose from the dead to justify you before God. If you do, please cry out to the Living God, something like this (in your own words):

*"God, I want to know you. I see that my sin broke the connection with you. But I see that you purposefully died for my sins and rose from the dead, making a bridge of connection. I'm sorry for my sins, I turn away from them now in anticipation of coming to know you. Please forgive me and please come into my heart today. In Jesus' name, amen."*

If you prayed this prayer just now, we would love to hear about it to rejoice with you. Please email us at bridge.trilogy@gmail.com as we would love to celebrate with you and encourage you in your new life walking with Jesus.

If this book leaves you with even a small sense of hope, that Jesus has restored the bridge through His death and resurrection, that grace is stronger than guilt, then I'm profoundly grateful.

**If you enjoyed this book, would you please leave a review on Amazon?** Your reviews help other readers discover this story and it would mean a lot to me.

**The Bridge Trilogy continues!** Watch for the next two books in this series:

- Book 2: *The Living Bridge*

- *Book 3: The Eternal Bridge*

**Connect with me:** The best way to stay updated is to follow me in my writing portal on Substack at https://mikecleveland.substack.com/, where I write posts and share updates. Paid Substack subscribers receive free signed copies of each new book I release (one per quarter).

Thank you for spending time with this story.

With hope and gratitude,

**Mike Cleveland**

# CHAPTER SEVENTEEN

# Before The Bridge Was Built

## A PREVIEW OF THE LIVING BRIDGE

You've witnessed the climactic sacrifice that restored the bridge and reunited two shores. But what led to that moment? Who was Geshriel before he became the keystone?

"The Living Bridge", Book 2 in the Bridge Trilogy series, takes you back to the months before the ultimate sacrifice, revealing the untold stories of five broken souls who experienced the broken bridge, but then encountered a carpenter with soil on his hands and compassion in his eyes.

Discover how the true bridge was built—not just with stone, but with presence, pain, and powerful self-giving love. This story covers the time period after the collapse of the Great Bridge through the self-giving sacrifice, and resurrection of Geshriel.

The following is Chapter One of The Living Bridge, offered here as a preview.

\*\*\*

### The Silenced Voice

From Torment to Testimony

The demons began whispering to her at dawn, as they always did.

*"You are worthless. Forgotten. Better if you'd never been born,"* said the demons, who
went by the name "Legion."

Mary pressed her palms against her ears, but the whispers lived inside her skull, weaving
through her thoughts like poison through water. She sat hunched on the rocky shore of
the Vitae River, the same lonely stretch she returned to each morning when the voices
pulled her from sleep.

The broken bridge loomed overhead, its jagged eastern fragment casting shadows
across the water. How fitting, she thought. A broken bridge for a broken woman.

*Look at you. Even the bridge has more worth; at least it once served a purpose.*

She rocked back and forth, humming an old song her mother had sung, trying to
drown out the relentless voices of the demons. But they only grew louder, more insistent,
feeding on her attempts to resist them.

*Remember when you thought you could create beauty? When you thought your hands
could weave light itself into cloth? Such arrogance.*

The memory stung because it had once been true. Mary the Weaver, they'd called
her, and the name had been spoken with respect. Her patterns had been unlike any
other, intricate designs that seemed to capture the very essence of living things. Gardens
bloomed across her tapestries. Birds took flight in threads of gold and silver. Even the
bridge itself had inspired one of her greatest works: a hanging that showed the eastern
and western shores united in perfect harmony.

*All gone now. All ruined. Just like everything you touch.*

From the village path above came the sound of approaching feet. Mary didn't need
to look to know what would happen next. The footsteps would slow, then stop entirely
as the owner spotted her. A whispered word of warning to any companions. A hurried
change of direction.

"There she is," came a woman's voice. It was Miriam, who had once commissioned a
wedding hanging from her. "The mad one, demon possessed. Quick, children, don't look
at her. Don't let her curse fall on you."

Mary glanced up to see Miriam shepherding her two young ones away from the
riverbank, their small faces twisted with curiosity and fear. The children had grown since
she'd last seen them clearly. How long had it been since she'd really noticed anything
outside her own torment?

*Even children know what you are. Cursed. Possessed. Unclean. A cautionary tale.*

She turned back to the water, watching the morning light dance across its surface. Once, she would have seen patterns in that light, inspiration for her next weaving. Now she saw only the endless flow of water, carrying debris away from the broken bridge toward the distant sea.

*Stay here with us, Mary. We're the only ones who understand your pain. The only ones who will never leave you.*

The voices spoke truth, in their twisted way. Everyone else had abandoned her. But the voices... they'd been faithful companions through every dark hour.

***

*Tell us the story again. Tell us how we came to be friends.*

Mary closed her eyes, the memory rising like bile in her throat. But the voices demanded their entertainment, and she'd learned that resistance only made them crueler.

It had been three and a half years ago. She'd been Mary the Weaver then, proud of her skill, in love with Jonah the carpenter from Westshore. They'd planned to marry as soon as harvest ended, to build a home and make a life on the eastern side where she could continue her craft.

She'd been working on her masterpiece, a wedding hanging that would tell their story. Threads of sky blue for Jonah's eyes, warm brown for his skilled hands, silver for the moonlight under which he'd proposed. The pattern showed two figures meeting in the center of a bridge, hands reaching toward each other across flowing water.

*You were so happy then. So foolishly happy.*

When the day arrived for their final wedding preparations, a storm had come. Rain poured, lightning split the sky as she stood at the window, calling to him across the widening floodplain. He should have waited. The river had already swallowed half the road.

But Jonah had been eager, impatient to start their life together.

She'd seen him leave the safety of higher ground, boots sloshing through the rising current, gripping a lantern against the wind.

She'd watched him vanish in a sudden surge, just gone, swept away in the flash flood before she could scream his name.

*You stood at this very spot for hours, waiting for him to surface. Calling his name until your voice gave out. But he never came back, did he?*

The grief had been unbearable, a physical weight pressing down on her chest until she could barely breathe. For days, she'd functioned like a sleepwalker, going through the motions of living while feeling hollow inside.

It was on the seventh night after his death, as she sat vigil by his grave, that despair had finally overwhelmed her. She'd fallen to her knees and cried out to anyone who might be listening; God, angels, demons, she no longer cared.

"Take this pain away," she'd sobbed. "I can't bear it anymore. Please, anything to make it stop."

*And we answered.*

The first voice had come as a whisper so soft she'd mistaken it for wind.

*"Poor Mary. Such suffering. We can help you forget."*

"Who's there?" she'd asked, looking around the empty graveyard.

*"Friends,"* came the reply. *"We know what it's like to lose everything. Let us ease your burden."*

She should have run. Should have recognized the danger. But the pain had been too great, and the offer of relief too tempting.

"Yes," she'd whispered. "Please."

The voices had kept their promise, for a time. The crushing grief had faded to a dull ache. She'd been able to function, to eat, even to sleep. But gradually, she'd realized the cure was worse than the disease.

*We didn't lie. We took away your pain. We gave you purpose.*

The voices had taken more than pain. They'd stolen her joy, her hope, her very sense of self. What had begun as whispered comfort had become constant criticism. They'd driven away friends who tried to help, convinced her that everyone's concern was mere pity or obligation.

*Remember Sarah? How she offered to let you stay with her family? We protected you from that humiliation.*

Her sister, Sarah, had indeed reached out after Mary began speaking to herself in public, after she'd started arriving late and disheveled to her weaving commissions. But the voices had whispered poisonous interpretations of every kindness.

*"She just feels sorry for you. She'll grow tired of your burden soon enough. Better to spare yourself the inevitable rejection."*

One by one, they'd isolated her from everyone who cared. Her father's shame at the public meeting had been the final blow, the public declaration that she was beyond redemption.

*See how they cast you out? Even your own father couldn't bear to look at you. We told you this would happen.*

The voices laughed, that sound like breaking glass that had become the soundtrack to her existence.

*But we remained. Through every rejection, every whispered curse, every crossed street to avoid you, we stayed. We are your truest friends, Mary. Your only real companions.*

***

"Peace, Mary."

The voice came from behind her, gentle and utterly unafraid. She spun around, heart hammering. A man stood on the path above the riverbank; ordinary in appearance, with kind eyes and dusty traveling clothes.

*Warning! Warning! He sees too much! He threatens our arrangement!*

The voices in her head shrieked suddenly, no longer whispered but screaming. Mary clutched her temples, doubling over in pain. Their panic was unlike anything she'd experienced before; raw, primal terror.

*Send him away! He doesn't belong here! He'll ruin everything!*

"Don't," she gasped to the man. "Don't come closer. I'm not... I can't control them. They don't want you here."

But the man, Geshriel, she somehow knew his name without being told, descended the rocky slope with calm steps. As he drew near, the voices grew more frantic, their whispers becoming a cacophony of rage and fear.

*He wants to separate us! He wants to leave you alone with your pain again! Fight him! Resist!*

"Mary the Weaver," Geshriel said with respect, settling beside her on the rocks as if he'd done so a hundred times before. "Daughter of Abram. Beloved of the Most High."

The words hit her like physical blows. Such respect. And no one had called her by her father's name in years. No one had called her beloved... ever.

*Don't listen! He speaks honeyed lies! We know the truth about you!*

From the path above came urgent shouts. "Master! Don't go near her; she's possessed! Dangerous!"

Geshriel didn't even glance up. His attention remained fixed on Mary, his presence somehow both gentle and immovably strong. There was something in his eyes; not the fear or pity she'd grown accustomed to, but a deep, abiding love that seemed to see straight through to her true self.

*He knows what we are! He knows our names! Our purposes! He threatens the very order we've built!*

The voices cut off abruptly as Geshriel reached out, not to touch her but simply to let his hand rest near hers on the stone between them.

For the first time in three and a half years, Mary's mind was quiet.

"How?" she whispered, tears streaming down her face.

"Because I know who you really are," Geshriel replied, his voice carrying a tenderness that made her heart ache. "Not what inhabits you, but who you truly are. Mary the Weaver, daughter of Abram, who once wove patterns so beautiful they seemed to contain light itself. Mary, who loved Jonah so deeply that even death couldn't diminish it."

Mary burst into tears of remembrance and stared at him in wonder. "I don't remember how to be her anymore."

"She never left. She was only hidden beneath their lies." Geshriel gaze held hers steadily. "You are precious, Mary. Loved beyond measure. Worthy of healing, worthy of hope, worthy of the life you were created to live."

*Lies! All lies! Remember your failures! Remember your shame!*

But even as the voices returned with their familiar accusations, they seemed thinner somehow, less substantial in the face of Geshriel's unwavering love.

***

The voices returned with a vengeance, howling now, no longer trying to whisper their poison but screaming their claim with desperate fury.

*She belongs to us! We found her first! We comforted her when no one else would! We have rights! Legal claims!*

Mary doubled over again, her body convulsing as the battle raged within her. "Don't let them take me back," she pleaded, grasping Geshriel's robe. "Please, I can't bear it anymore."

Geshriel stood, his ordinary appearance suddenly transformed. Authority radiated from him like heat from a fire, but underneath it was something even more powerful; a love so pure, so complete, that it made the demons' possessiveness look like the pale shadow it was.

*You don't understand! She invited us in! She welcomed us! She chose us over the pain!*

"I understand perfectly," Geshriel said, his voice carrying absolute command while remaining infinitely gentle. "You offered her a counterfeit comfort when her heart was broken. But I provide her something far greater; true healing, complete restoration, perfect love that drives out fear."

He turned to Mary, his eyes blazing with compassion. "Mary the Weaver, daughter of Abram, this is what I came to do; not just for you, but for every broken heart, every tormented soul, everyone who has been deceived into believing they are beyond hope."

*No! She is ours! Our prize! Our dwelling place!*

"What I do for Mary today," Geshriel continued, speaking to both her and the demons, "I will one day do for all creation. Every chain will be broken. Every prison door opened. Every captive set free." His voice rose with prophetic power. "Death itself will lose its claim, and love will triumph over every darkness."

Mary felt something shift deep within her soul; not just the promise of personal freedom, but a glimpse of something cosmic, universal. This man's love wasn't just for her; it was for everyone who suffered, everyone who was lost, everyone who had given up hope.

*We will not go! We will not—*

"Come out of her," Geshriel commanded, his voice like thunder. "The One who created light from darkness comes to reclaim what was stolen."

The struggle was fierce but brief. Mary felt the darkness fighting, clawing, desperate to maintain its hold. The demons threw every accusation they could muster—her failures, her guilt, her moments of weakness. But none of it could stand against the blazing love that surrounded her.

*This isn't over! We will find others! We will—*

"Come out of her, and enter her no more!"

With a final shriek of rage and defeat, the voices fled, leaving behind only blessed silence and the overwhelming sense of being truly, completely loved.

Mary gasped, her mind suddenly, startlingly her own again. The constant background noise of whispered accusations was gone. The weight that had pressed down on her thoughts lifted. She looked around with eyes that truly saw for the first time in years.

The river sparkled in the morning sun. Birds sang in the trees above. The same river that had once taken Jonah now shimmered as if it had never known sorrow. The very air seemed fresher, cleaner, alive with possibility. But more than that; she felt clean inside, as if every stain on her soul had been washed away.

"I'm free," she whispered, then louder, laughing with pure joy. "I'm free!"

Geshriel smiled, his face radiant with shared happiness. "Welcome home, Mary. The old has passed away. Behold, all things are new."

***

As the initial rush of freedom settled into steady peace, Mary looked at her healer with wonder. "Why? Why did you help me when everyone else turned away?"

Geshriel's expression grew serious, touched with a sadness she couldn't fully understand. "Because you are loved, Mary. And what I've done for you is a glimpse of what love can accomplish."

He helped her to her feet, his touch warm and steadying. "The enemy wants everyone to believe that some souls are beyond redemption, that some chains can never be broken. But that's a lie. The same power that freed you can free anyone; will free everyone who calls on my name."

"I don't understand," Mary said, though something in her spirit seemed to recognize a truth too large for words.

"One day you will." Geshriel's eyes held depths she couldn't fathom. "You will see the ultimate triumph of love over hatred, light over darkness, life over death itself. And you will understand that what happened to you today is just the beginning."

He paused, studying her face as if memorizing it. "Your healing is a sign, Mary. A foretaste of the restoration that's coming. When that day arrives, every chain will be broken; not just for individuals, but for all creation."

The words sent a strange chill through her, part anticipation, part dread. "What do you mean?"

But Geshriel was already moving back toward the path, gesturing for her to follow. "Come. Let's show the village what the love of God looks like when it sets captives free."

Mary hesitated, familiar fear rising. "They won't accept me. Too much has happened. Too much pain caused."

"Healing isn't just for you, Mary," Geshriel said gently. "It's for everyone who witnesses it. Your restoration will give them hope for their own."

Together they climbed from the riverbank to the village path. As they emerged onto the main road, a group of early morning traders stopped in their tracks. Their faces registered shock, then disbelief, then something like awe.

"Mary?" one of them whispered—Ezekiel, who had once bought her finest work for his daughter's dowry. "Is that... Mary the Weaver?"

For the first time in three and a half years, Mary stood straight, looked them in the eye, and spoke with a clear, strong voice. "Yes. I am Mary, daughter of Abram. And I am healed."

As word spread through Eastlight, people emerged from their homes to witness the impossible. The woman they'd written off as irredeemably broken walked among them whole, her eyes bright with purpose instead of madness.

And beside her walked the teacher whose power was becoming impossible to ignore; the one who could restore even the most shattered soul. The one whose destiny, Mary sensed with growing certainty, would not only heal individuals but transform all things. The one who would show the world that love truly was stronger than death.

And Mary, once broken, now walked with light in her hands again—Mary the Weaver, daughter of Abram.

www.ingramcontent.com/pod-product-compliance
Lightning Source LLC
Chambersburg PA
CBHW032144170626
46808CB00006B/2363